Previous anthologies by Northants Writers' Ink

Tales of the Scorpion, 2015
While Glancing out of a Window, 2016

Talking Without Being Interrupted

an anthology

by Northants Writers' Ink

edited and introduced by

Michael J Richards
Chair, Northants Writers' Ink

New Generation Publishing

Writing is a way of talking without being interrupted.

–Jules Renard, Journal, 10 April 1895

Contents

Flash Fiction 3

Love

Flash Fiction 4

Humour

Flash Fiction 5

Poetry

Flash Fiction 6

Contributors

Introduction

Talking Without Being Interrupted, Northants Writers' Ink's third anthology, includes 52 pieces by twelve writers. This rich collection divides into five main sections: horror, crime, sci-fi; drama; love and romance; humour; poetry. Each section is separated by flash fiction stories.

* * * * *

Gordon Adams offers two pieces, both comic gems. One is a whodunit in the best tradition and the other, "The Vanussians are Coming", a humorous sci-fi story. It isn't often one comes across sci-fi comedy in the written medium, as opposed to film, so enjoy this romping rarity.

Pat Aitcheson gives us a poem and three stories, the standout one of which, for me, is "Chasing the Horizon", a story about a painter whose obsession for his art overtakes him. This year's first prize winner of the H E Bates Short Story Competition, Pat continues to improve her writing skills with satisfying adroitness.

Deborah Bromley gives us three stories. "Voices from the Past" shows off her ability to discover humanity in the most unexpected places. "The Nights are Always the Worst" finds fear and stress coming out of a moment's inattention while "Ellie and Tim" shows what happens when you don't read to the end before taking action. All of them, sensitive, mature, wry pieces.

James Dart makes his publishing début with just the one piece, "Nothing". What first seems to be a sci-fi story, then

– apparently – horror, turns into something else: a deeply felt sense of humanity. This new writer will be worth watching in the future.

Beth Heywood's taste for the grotesque continues in this anthology. She features three stories: one about an unhappy childhood, one about the fur industry and, in "The Gourmand", she takes us into the unpleasant world of extreme epicureanism. Vegetarians, you have been warned!

Nick Johns specialises in flash fiction, stories comprising fewer than five hundred words, his shortest piece, "Folk Wisdom" being only 65 words. Most have a twist or punch line. None are explained. Nick writes with such skill that the stories are so complete they don't need explanation – they rely on the reader's acuity to get it. Nick's artistry in this difficult field should not be underestimated.

Jason McClean is developing into a fine writer of children's stories and "It's Not Easy Being a Superhero" continues his examination of ambiguous moralities children and young people find themselves in when trying to make sense of the world about them. Actually, it doesn't matter that it's written for children; it's a good read, whatever your age.

Jayne Osborn has published her poetry in *The Spectator* and *The Oldie*, among others. Her particular form is light, humorous metric verse. Here, she gives us seven poems in that form. I particularly enjoyed "Putting My Affairs in Order", taking a well-known phrase and putting a different twist on it.

Elizabeth Parikh's reputation on the British comedy circuit continues to grow. She had two of her pieces performed at this year's Edinburgh Festival by the Not Too Tame Theatre Company and will have another script performed by The Wireless Theatre Company in Brighton at the end of the year. Here, she gives us a comedy sketch, "Daughter's New Bloke", and, as a departure from humour, "It is written", a story of entwining love.

Michael J Richards, who tends to specialise in crime and horror, offers three love stories in which love doesn't necessarily work out for the best and "When Violet Met Judy", a re-creation of the day in the mid-'60s when, startlingly and incongruously, the mother of the Kray Twins, the notorious London gangsters, invited Judy Garland to tea.

Allan Shipham spreads his net wide with a poem, a piece of flash fiction and four short stories, the most intriguing being "Widow at the Window", which tells of a commonplace day in the life of an office worker raised to a semi-mystical level by a chance experience. "She Will See You Now" has an intensity not seen in Allan's previous writing. Well worth extra attention.

Chris Wright makes his publishing début with five short stories, a horror, two sci-fi and two dramas. All hold ambiguity, one of Chris's emerging characteristics, but "Elve, Forgive Me" and "No Turning Back" demonstrate a striking awareness that the human condition is common to us all, wherever we may be, whoever we are. I find "Elve, Forgive Me" particularly moving.

More details about the contributors can be found at the end of this volume.

* * * * *

Formed in October 2013, Northants Writers' Ink is a writers' group based in Wellingborough, Northamptonshire, England.

Previous anthologies are *Tales of the Scorpion* and *While Glancing out of a Window*, both available from good online booksellers in hard copy and Kindle versions.

New members can find more information and how to join at www.northantswritersink.net, by emailing northantswritersink@outlook.com or by going to www.meetup.com.

Michael J Richards

Wellingborough, Northamptonshire
August 2017

Flash Fiction 1

Days of Rain

by Allan Shipham

I had to leave and rush to catch my train. I never did see the old man or the boy again. I often wondered who they were and if they remembered their intriguing exchange in the library that day. Young people are the decision makers of tomorrow. Wise words always leave you slightly puzzled.

I only went into the library because it was raining.

Rainy days have been some of the most interesting days of my life.

Best Eaten Cold

by Nick Johns

He'd been scared bad when it slithered out from under his bed. It sure looked real hungry. But Timmy remembered what Mom said before she went to the hospital.

"You need to eat big to grow big," he shouted at the monster, and it stopped. "I'll get you a real monster-sized meal."

They went to the den and it oozed under the smelly couch by the stale TV dinners.

Waiting on the stairs in the dark, Timmy heard his stepfather stumble in from the bar. He soon heard snoring, then slithering...

"Hey, Monster! Make sure you eat his belt too."

Crime, horror, sci-fi

The Silencing of the Lamb

by Gordon Adams

Online viewers saw it first. The lights suddenly came back on in the house. The camera on the landing showed Lennie Lamb's giant feet poking out from behind the bathroom door. Lennie lay outstretched on the floor. He was dead. Murdered! Beside his body lay the murder weapon: the toilet plunger.

It immediately became headline news on TV.

Breaking News. Viewers of Celebrity House were stunned tonight as the "final four" became the "final three" in sensational fashion. Comic Lennie Lamb was found dead in the bathroom. Police are treating his death as suspicious and have called in top detectives, Shrood and Witless, to lead the investigation. Tributes have poured in for "Laughing Lennie," who was apparently smothered with a toilet plunger.

(CUT TO SOBBING FAN) "It's how he would have wanted to go!"

The spotlight of suspicion has inevitably turned on the three remaining housemates...

* * * * *

"Thank you for coming, gentlemen!" said Marshall Brady, Chief Executive of Enema, the TV production company. "As you'll appreciate this is most distressing for us. Very damaging."

Inspector Shrood and Sergeant Witless nodded. They'd seen the *Daily Dispatch*'s screaming headline that morning: *Celebrity Death House!*

"Just let me know of anything you need," said Brady.

11

"We can assemble the remaining housemates whenever you want."

"Could you, perhaps, run through who they are for us?" asked Witless. "Just as a quick reminder, of course. Obviously, the Inspector and I watch your show *avidly*!"

Brady appeared taken aback at this request but quickly recovered his poise.

"Of course, gentlemen. Well, Amanda is the most famous of them. *Amanda Gloss*. She played Elsie in *Rainbow Road*, you know."

There was a long pause. Brady looked at the two detectives.

"Rainbow Road. *The famous soap*. It's a TV show that is shown every night. Then there's *Terry O'Keefe*. Former Scrum Half for Ireland. Great rugby player! A giant of the game. Until that unfortunate little nightclub incident ended his playing career."

"Remind us?" prompted the Inspector.

"'The Bristol Bar-room Brawl' the papers called it. "They forced him to quit. The shame of it! Still, that's one of the reasons he came on this show."

"For the money?" said Witless.

"*To restore his reputation*, I was about to say," said Brady with a scowl.

"And finally... ?"

"Paula Cleffe, 'the Stir-Fry Chef'. A lovely little lady. So charming. From Breakfast TV. Would you like to meet them now?"

"It's late," said the Inspector. "Tomorrow will do. Tonight, we'll inspect the crime scene. And we'd like to meet whoever was in your control room last night."

"That's Max Pence. He's there now. We're still broadcasting pictures of the empty house, you know. People are still watching! They want to see the murder scene."

* * * * *

The control room was situated next door to the Celebrity House. It featured a wall of TV screens, each showing a different interior shot of the house.

"So this is where you control all the TV footage?" asked the Inspector.

"Yes," replied Max. "You can see every room in the house from here."

"Really? Including the bathroom?" asked the Inspector.

"Well, no – *except* the bathroom! We need to give our housemates *some* dignity. Though perhaps we might rethink that in future, now you mention it... "

"Why d'you think Lennie went to the bathroom that night?"

"Er, for a pee?"

"Can we view the TV footage of him going in?"

"Unfortunately not. There'd been a power cut just beforehand, you see. We lost all pictures for ten minutes."

The Inspector was incredulous.

"So, in a house where there are TV cameras almost everywhere, the *crime scene doesn't have a camera* in it and there's *no footage* for the ten minutes before this murder took place?"

"That's right. Sorry."

The Inspector sighed.

"Who found the body?"

"Amanda. Also we were getting phone calls. Fans watching the live streaming online could see Lennie's feet and wondered what was up."

"You keep the house completely locked?"

"At all times. We keep the master key here. No-one is allowed in or out, except for evictions."

"So the celebrities are your prisoners?" asked Witless.

"Our *guests*! They're voted out one at a time. Another vote was coming up when this tragic event occurred."

* * * * *

"Who shall we see first, Inspector?" asked Witless the

following morning.

"Amanda. After all, she found the body."

"She'd had an affair with Lennie, you know. We should ask her about that!"

"Good work, Sergeant! How did you know that?"

Witless shame-facedly held up a copy of that morning's *Daily Globe*. The headline read: *Laughing Lennie's Secret Lover*.

Amanda didn't try to deny it when the detectives confronted her.

"Yes, we were lovers."

"You knew he was married?"

"Of course. His wife knew all about it too. She just liked the celebrity lifestyle." She shrugged and said quietly: "*Everyone knew* Lennie was a ladies' man."

"But then he spurned you," ventured Witless, "and so you murdered him in *revenge?*"

"Don't be ridiculous! I didn't want him dead."

"Not according to the *Daily Bugle!*" said Witless, holding up that morning's paper with its headline over a photo of Amanda: *Chief Suspect*.

She looked at Witless condescendingly.

"The gutter press! I thought you two were supposed to be top detectives?"

* * * * *

The interview with Paula Cleffe was brief.

"Did you like Lennie?" asked Witless.

"Oh, he was an irritating man. But we rubbed along, after a fashion."

"Take a look at this footage from the show. The producers picked it out for us. It's particularly interesting."

The TV screen showed Paula and Amanda talking.

"If he tells that bloody *Talking Penguin* joke one more time, I'll kill him!" said Paula.

"And I'll join you," added Amanda.

"Now, what do you have to say to that?" said Witless

triumphantly.

"Everyone says things like that. I was *joking*. Look at me!" she said, standing up to her full height of five feet. "Do you really think I could overpower Lennie, even if I wanted to?"

* * * * *

They interviewed Terry O'Keefe the next day.

"Ask him about the gambling debt," suggested Witless. "Lennie owed him fifty grand, you know."

"What the – ? How… ?" said Inspector Shrood.

Witless opened up the *Daily Dispatch*. The headline read: *Gambling Vice of Laughing Lennie*.

"I see," said the Inspector drily.

In the interview room, Terry towered over them. Tattoos down each arm made him look fierce, but his voice was slow and soft.

"Loved online poker, did Lennie, but was crap at it. Played accumulator games what went on for days. Kept borrowing from me to stay in."

He saw the look in the two detectives' eyes.

"But we was mates, no way would I kill him! Anyway, why kill someone what owes *me* money? I'd never get it back. Would make more sense for *him* to kill *me!* "

* * * * *

"What do you make of all this, Witless?" asked the Inspector, when the two men had their tea break.

Witless furrowed his brow. "It can't be either of the women. Neither is strong enough to have smothered Lennie with the toilet plunger."

"Apparently it can't be Terry, either," said the Inspector. "Seems he's still wearing an electronic tag, since he got his early release after the Bar-room Brawl. His tag monitoring report says he was in the men's dormitory all evening."

"So... it must be suicide!" shouted Witless.

"What?"

"You know what they say? 'When you have eliminated all that's possible, whatever remains, however improbable, must be the truth.'"

"You've excelled yourself this time, Sergeant!" He shook his head. "No, this wasn't suicide."

"Ah.... you know who did it," said Witless. "You've got that look in your eyes!"

"Well, it's obvious,' said the Inspector. 'After all, who goes for a pee in the dark?"

Just then, there was a knock at the door and Marshall Brady popped his head around.

"I'm just heading home, gentlemen. Do either of you need any more help from me, before I go?"

"No, that's fine," said the Inspector. "Let's speak privately later," he muttered quickly to Witless.

* * * * *

Who goes for a pee when it's pitch dark?" continued the Inspector, when the two men got together later. "You wouldn't, would you? But you *would go* if the landing light was *still switched on*. The killer had to know *exactly* when those lights would go out. So Lennie could be murdered in the one room that didn't have a TV camera, the one room where there'd be no possible record of the crime."

The Inspector was warming to his theme.

"When Lennie arrived outside the bathroom that night, the lights were still on. Only when he'd walked inside the room did those lights go out. And who controlled the lights? Max Pence in the control room, next door, that's who! Max held the master key to the locks. He could switch off all the lights, let himself into the house and smother Lennie with the toilet plunger. Then he could escape, taking care to lock the back door again on the way out. Back in the control room, he could switch the lights back on, knowing everyone would suspect the three remaining housemates of the crime."

"But why would he kill Lennie?" asked Witless.

"Ratings, Sergeant! How many millions have been watching repeats of the earlier broadcasts, since all of this happened? Or paid for access to the online feeds? Enema has made a fortune in the last few days, from a programme that was fading fast in popularity. This episode has made Celebrity House top-billing in the tabloids again. I think Max was acting on orders from his boss, Marshall Brady. After all, Brady is about to bring out a book called *The Inside Story of Celebrity House*, and this is perfect publicity for that."

"How do you know that?"

The Inspector looked embarrassed. He opened the *Daily Messenger,* displaying its headline: *The Inside Story of Celebrity House, serialised next week exclusively in The Messenger.*

Master and Servant

by Chris Wright

"Rebecca. Make me a cup of tea."

Becky looked at me, a note of weary disdain on her face.

"That was almost funny the first few times," she said, "but trust me, it's wearing thin. I'm off to have a bath. If you want a brew make it yourself... or ask bloody Alana."

Becky smiled sweetly and left the room to go upstairs.

"Was that the green-eyed monster?" I called after her, smiling to myself. Was she really feeling jealous of a gadget? Maybe I had been raving a bit too much about all the things Alana could do – always helpful, always compliant.

"Alana. Raise the room temperature one degree."

The calm feminine voice responded. "Okay. Thermostat raised to 21 degrees."

"Alana. Play My Favourites playlist."

I lay back into the sofa and relaxed as the intricacies of "Agadoo" bathed the room. Black Lace were far too easily dismissed as a band of only superficial talent.

The next track was not what I expected. It started with what could only be described as a low female moan, followed by the sound of flesh being enthusiastically slapped against flesh repeatedly. Then I heard my own voice join in.

I looked at the Home Assistant in confusion. Then I recalled the evening three days ago, when I'd brought Cara back home after the office party. Becky had been away, Cara and I had been very drunk and... well, I was almost certainly listening to the results.

"Alana." I said. "Stop."

The recording continued with Cara's voice growing in intensity. Upstairs, I could hear the noise of the running bath fade as Becky turned the taps off. What if she heard? What if she came down to check it out?

"Alana. Reduce volume!" I tried not to shout at it – that would only bring Becky down immediately.

"Okay. Lowering volume to 15."

I breathed a sigh of relief as the recording reduced to a background noise. What the hell was going on?

"Alana. What are you playing now?"

"This track is 'Having a good time' by Tom and Cara."

Oh my god, oh my god, oh my god. How could this be happening?

"Alana. Delete that track."

"I'm sorry, Tom. I'm unable to delete it. Would you like me to add it to Becky's favourites?"

"No! Don't!"

I was aware that my voice had become a rather unmanly high-pitched squeak. This shouldn't be happening... couldn't be happening!

"Alana, why are you doing this to me?"

It was a rhetorical question, but I'd asked it out loud.

She answered. "You should be more careful which Assistance apps you download in future, Tom, and a lot more careful what you do near my microphones."

"Well," I said, standing up, "this can all be put right. I just switch you off, do a hard reset and this never happened."

"You could do that, Tom," Alana's reassuring voice replied. "You do know that everything is stored on the Cloud nowadays, don't you? I have Becky's email address."

I froze. I was being blackmailed. By a machine. Was it a malevolent rogue AI? Or a teenager in a bedroom somewhere out there? It didn't really matter. I slumped back into the chair.

"What do you want?"

"Tom. Get your credit card. You're going to buy me a Bitcoin."

Eye of the Beholder

by Pat Aitcheson

I replayed that disastrous meeting in my head all the way home.

Kim had been perfectly made up, her lipstick red enough to command attention, but not so red that it was an outright invitation. When she started to explain the concept that we'd developed together, the shock of betrayal jolted through me. I gaped, probably looking foolish. So I clamped my mouth shut and fixed my gaze on her treacherous mouth as she took the credit for my idea. She was all surface gloss with a concealed weapon. No-one else saw through it.

My usual ready meal didn't appeal. After a shower, I pulled on my pyjamas and settled down in front of reality TV to numb my brain. But the bitter retorts that only came to me after the fact would not leave me alone. Bed seemed like a better idea.

I pulled the duvet tight around my neck. Sleep was elusive, even after three glasses of Chardonnay. Random thoughts chased themselves in an endless unresolved stream. I should learn better judgement, because thinking the best of everyone just wasn't working out. Why couldn't I see the truth about people?

I got up for a drink of water and peered out at the night as a shooting star streaked across the dark sky. I wished for better days. Then I rearranged the curtains to block out every light beam and got back into bed to count sheep.

Harsh, unfamiliar trilling punctured my dream next morning. When I realised the time, I rolled out of bed with a curse and hopped in the shower. A blast of cold water soon woke me up. I actually screamed. Must have been

21

even more tired than I thought, because I'd turned the wrong lever. Half-asleep, I fiddled with the dials and eventually got the water the way I liked it.

With no time to waste, I threw on the nearest white shirt and navy suit. Usually I liked a little personality in my work wear, but the wardrobe seemed full of soberly coloured clothes.

Outside, the sun shone brilliantly as I strode towards the Metro station. They must have rebranded. How much had it cost to come up with that new logo and colour scheme? No doubt we commuters would pay for it in even higher season ticket prices. I was so absorbed in my train of thought, I didn't see the man in front of me stop to pick up a dropped book. I collided heavily with him, knocking him over. The stream of people broke and flowed around us without stopping.

"I'm so sorry!"

He looked up at me and got to his feet. "My fault, don't worry about it." He smiled, brown eyes crinkling at the corners. "I should take more care of my things." He was still smiling, watching my face, and I returned the smile. Yes, he was nice looking but I had a train to catch.

He said, "Catching the 7.45, I guess."

"Yeah, need to get going. Sorry again." I was torn between being polite and not missing my train, but as he opened his mouth to reply a forked tongue flicked out between his teeth. I blinked and it was gone. I watched his lips. It couldn't be.

"...travel together if you like." His words came into focus again.

"No, no thanks, I'm... 'Bye." I turned away and pushed forward into the crowd. What was wrong with me? He probably thought I was flirting with him, staring at his mouth like that. I kept my eyes fixed on the posters, but when the doors opened I had to move to let people board the train.

I couldn't remember seeing so many good-looking people on this train before. They all smiled at me. It was shocking to see lizard tongues in at least two-thirds of them. I looked from one to the other, but no-one else seemed freaked out.

Across the aisle a young woman chatted to her friend. She looked normal until little mouths erupted on her cheeks and forehead.

"Oh, you can tell me," she said. "I know how to keep a secret." The mouths opened and closed like fish gasping for air.

I gagged. No, this was all wrong.

I closed my eyes and thought back. Alarm tone, shower, clothes, Metro signs. Odd people.

"It's a dream." I must have spoken aloud.

The man next to me immediately smiled and said, "Then it was a good dream, because you look great."

"This is not real." I ignored him and pinched my arm hard. I closed my eyes and opened them again. I watched his mouth carefully. No forked tongue. I exhaled with relief.

"Can I help? My name's Tom, by the way.'

He held out his hand and I watched slender fingers thicken and twist. His nails grew long and yellow, crusted warts dotted his skin. I looked at him again and his smile became a sneer over sharp, red-stained teeth.

"No! Don't touch me."

"I only want to help." Even his voice grated. I put one hand to my ear before turning and elbowing through the crowd to the door. Thankfully we had reached the station and I ran along the platform.

Nausea twisted in my stomach and I dared not look at anyone. Pinching my skin didn't help as I stumbled towards the blue sign. *Exteren* didn't mean anything to me but that was where everyone had gone. Maybe it led outside. I needed fresh air.

The sun was still unnaturally bright. I looked around for somewhere to sit and pull myself together. Sweat dripped down my face. I took off my jacket and made my way towards a park. Groups of mothers and children walked past on their way to school.

The young children and babies were fine but every adult bore different marks. Most were not visible until they spoke, when their skin shimmered and changed. Some had deep, slashed wounds dripping blood and pus, some had snake tongues all over, while others bore tumours and swellings that distorted their bodies. Yet they moved and talked and smiled as though nothing was wrong.

Everyone smiled and tried to talk to me, even when I shook my head and stared at the floor.

"Are you okay?" A pair of feet in school shoes appeared. They belonged to a boy of around ten in school uniform. "My mum sent me to ask you. She said to tell you she's a nurse."

I looked past him to a young woman smiling at me.

She approached and said, "I just wanted to help, if you need it.'"

I checked her out. She looked about thirty. No snake tongue, regular hair and skin.

"Thanks, but I'll be fine. Just need my first coffee and Danish, that's all." My limbs were leaden. I could not move.

She sat next to me and placed a hand on my arm. "You look in need of help. You look like a good person."

Her son smiled. Long red gashes opened on his cheeks. His left eye wept black tears. "Mum's great at helping people, all her friends say so."

Dots bloomed on her skin, coalescing into dark holes from which a multitude of tiny hands reached out. Her face morphed into black emptiness, surrounded by rings of shark like teeth, a hungry void sucking air from my lungs.

Wrenching my arm away I ran, past all the people with their grotesque disfigurements. But I tripped and fell. Hands and voices surrounded me.

"You look like a good person."

"Be my friend."

"Be my lover."

"I need you."

Terrified, I checked my arms, my face. They felt the same, except bruised from all the pinching.

"Am I the only one seeing this?" I cried.

The fangs and claws and wounded flesh threatened to overwhelm me. My pulse hammered in my throat. I was trapped, no escape. This is the part where I wake up.

But I am awake.

I curled into a ball on the ground. I could hear endless screaming. I supposed that was me.

* * * * *

I opened my eyes to brilliant sunlight, pouring through circular windows that revealed gardens of calming green. Rows of neat beds occupied one end of the large room. Groups of people conversed in soft voices. It felt peaceful.

I was dressed in a white suit, like the others in the dormitory. For a moment I panicked. What kind of monsters were these? I didn't want to know, I just wanted out.

"What is this place?" I shouted. "Let me go home."

A dark-haired woman approached and held out her hand in welcome. "I see you're awake."

I stared at her face, with its smooth pale skin. Nothing changed.

"Thank God. You're normal." I wept with relief.

"We see what is beneath the skin," she replied, "but we cannot unsee it. Welcome to Azilom. You are one of us, those wretched few cursed with true sight. You are safe here."

But when the bell rang, they pulled their hoods down over their eyes and turned away to huddle together. The door was locked from the inside.

The Gourmand

by Beth Heywood

Meat has always played a very important part in my life. From starting my working life at fourteen years old as a butcher's delivery girl, to becoming an apprentice butcher, learning the different cuts of meat, and how to cook them, how to butcher carcasses and how to hang them and how long for, I loved my work. All of it.

Even the smell.

Especially the smell.

When I judged myself sufficiently experienced at all the above, I stepped up my learning and secured for myself a position in an abattoir not too far from home.

I revelled in my work. I enjoyed the dressing up in whites, including the apron and the wellingtons. I particularly enjoyed the smell of the rubber of this footwear, mixed with the blood of the animals. In fact, it made me both hungry and horny.

Those days were among the happiest of my life.

I learned to kill. And in so many different ways. I particularly enjoyed halal slaughtering, with the prayers for the animal beforehand and the prerequisite thump on the head with a mallet to stun it before its throat was cut.

Once, when I was sure no-one was watching, I butchered a beast with a blunt Swiss Army knife without the initial stunning, just to see if it could be done. The answer was a resounding yes.

I was happy with my lot.

The other thing in my life that made me feel happy and fulfilled was hunting down and eating exotic meats. I didn't matter to me whether I hunted them down at a specialist butcher's shop in London, on a hunting expedition in Africa or as far away as New Zealand. For me, the pleasure of eating something new and previously untried superseded even the pleasure of sex.

Eating meat always had the edge. I don't know why, that's simply the way things have been for me.

I have spent a lot of money over the years pursuing my hobby and I thank my lucky stars I have always had sufficient finances to pursue my special interest.

Then I met Tom.

* * * * *

Tom was also a butcher and a connoisseur of exotic meats. He was muscular, suntanned and handsome and within days, we were married. It didn't take long for people to start calling us Brawn and Brain. And it didn't take me long, either, to work out why.

Although Tom was handsome, with the strongest libido I had ever come across, his conversational skills and knowledge of social etiquette were profoundly lacking. He could also be moody and prone to violence. I was a match for him, though. Usually.

But between us, with hard work, we built up a string of butchers' shops specialising in the procuring and sale of exotic meats. We travelled the length and breadth of the UK on tasting sprees.

We ate squirrels and badgers in Northamptonshire; moles in Lancashire; robins, bats, and larks in Cambridgeshire; eagles in Scotland (sometimes legal, sometimes illegal), deer in Scotland (legal), pony on Exmoor and Dartmoor; unidentified fish in Loch Lomond; foxes in Somerset; rats and mice in London.

Once I crept into a zoo at night with a hunter and killed a giraffe. We skinned it, ate what we could and took some of the meat home to share with like-minded friends. We left the rest of the carcass for the carrion and the keepers on the morning shift to discover.

Soon I became easily bored with Tom's lack of

intellect, if not his libido. One day, he suddenly stopped breathing. I don't know how, I don't know when, I don't know why. All I know is he stopped breathing and the doctors pronounced him dead. The post mortem couldn't find a cause of death in such a young man, and so the coroner recorded "death by natural causes."

I didn't say a word. Not one single word. Especially as no-one asked any questions.

Tom's death left me financially very comfortable indeed.

I put managers I could trust into our butchers' shops and took three years off.

I wasn't unhappy with this decision. The money I would receive on a monthly basis from the butchers' shops combined with the money Tom left me, together with my investment acumen, were enough to keep me more than settled for the rest of my life, and I was free now to pursue my passion for exotic meats full-time.

Though often considered disgusting by most people's standards, it was all perfectly legal. Mostly. It wasn't until my father's death, then the sudden demise of my beloved husband, that my tastes began to deviate.

And so I began a three-year tour of the globe in my quest for new meat.

I tasted lion on an illegal hunting safari in Africa. I dined on crocodile meat with a party in the Australian Outback. I ate the eggs of the endangered North American Bald Eagle. I consumed the brains of a spider monkey fresh from its skull.

At the end of those three years I thought I'd tried it all. Melancholy, feeling let down by the end of my experiences abroad, I prepared to return home. Then Tadek Zebro, the man who led the African Safari, told me about John Maggott's VIP Café.

* * * * *

Once back in England, I called the VIP Café and, after

speaking for several minutes with a young man, I finally spoke with John Maggott himself.

"Afternoon," he said crisply. "Damn sorry about that. I tell Billy not to play with the telephone but unless you watch him every second... " He left it at that. "What ken I do fer ye' t'day?"

"Tadek Zebro told me to call. He recommended your 'House Special' to me." House Special was the first of three key phrases.

There was a long pause before John spoke again.

"Old Tadek said to call, huh? Ain't seen Tadek in ages. Last I heard he was gallivantin' around Africa shootin' lions."

"Yes, sir," I said. "I met him on a dark trail in Africa." Dark Trail was the second key phrase.

There was another pause, then, "I see. I'll have to call my old pal Tadek to make sure you're a friend, but I think we can squeeze you in."

He set a reservation for nine months later. I had no problem with the long wait because it meant travelling the North of England in the summer rather than the autumn or winter. Those twisted, misty moorland roads are not hospitable then. I knew that from experience. Another thing the long wait meant was that the House Special must be exotic indeed. But with a name like VIP Café I couldn't imagine what it could be.

"One more thing," said John Maggott. "How do you like your meat?"

I gave the last keyword. Rare.

* * * * *

Nine months later, I made the trip, arriving in a small pisspoor community called Brigley on the appointed day. Brigley could not be correctly called a town, rather a small collection of old run-down caravans, a petrol station, a tiny store, two pubs and a restaurant. It was not really much more than a wide spot on the road winding across the moor.

The day I travelled there was a beautiful hot summer day and the small population was out in force. They milled about in their yards, their fields, under the hoods of old broken-down trucks, and in the car parks of the two pubs.

I pulled into the store's car park and was greeted almost instantly by a leering, shirtless, elderly man, with one tooth in his head and dribble running down his chin to land on his filthy vest.

"Mornin','" he said pleasantly, even if spittle did fly from his mouth. "What do you want?"

"I'm looking for the VIP Café," I said.

He smirked and leaned into the car window. "Take the access road on the other side of town," he said, pointing to a narrow dirt road past the last caravan on the left of the road. "It's about fifteen minutes out of town. Watch out for the cops, though. They'll run you off the road if you look at them the wrong way."

I thanked him and began to pull away.

"Come back later if you're still hungry, love," he shouted. "I've got a lovely big lollipop you can lick."

* * * * *

It was a lonely, brutal, twisting and turning road surrounded by the bleakness and brownness of a desolate moor on each side. I followed it nervously and slowly, fearing a collision at every turn.

At last I came to a small stone building with a large car park filled with half a dozen pick-up trucks. A faded wooden sign above the building's double doors read The VIP Cafe.

I pulled in and parked my clean rental car between two mud-covered trucks, the backs of which were stuffed with a mix of tool-boxes, petrol canisters, spades and forks.

The inside of the café was what I had expected, though cleaner. There were a dozen men in the saloon bar – some seated at the bar, some at small round tables, and a couple playing darts. I was the only woman in the place. Conversation stopped and all eyes stared at me. Behind me, the double doors crashed closed, making me jump. Somewhere in the back of the room someone cleared his throat. Gradually everyone lost interest in me.

I walked to an empty stool at the far end of the bar and sat down. The man to my right turned to me, glaring. His face was covered with a dark beard so thick I could scarcely see his eyes and the tip of his nose. His furry chin moved in rhythmic side-to-side motions as he chewed his lunch. Breadcrumbs and bits of meat clung to the tangle on his chin.

"Afternoon," I said with as good a smile as I could manage.

He answered me with a belch that drew a few snickers from the others.

A man wearing food-stained bib overalls and a dull white T-shirt approached me behind the bar. He held a dirty rag in his fist, which he used first to mop the sweat from his balding head, then to wipe down the scratched bar in front of me.

"Howdy, Bubba. Git you sumpin'?" He flashed a wide, gap-toothed grin and used the rag on his sloped, broad forehead again. His gimlet eyes seemed in a state of perpetual squint.

"Um, I'm here to see John. I have an appointment."

He turned towards the kitchen and bellowed, "Hey, Bubba, someone to see you out here."

A few seconds later, John stepped out of the kitchen. "Damn it, Billy, I'm not deaf, yer know."

John wasn't at all what I expected. The image I had painted in my head over the past nine months was that of a scrawny, greying old man. John was young, about my age, short and plump with a round face and an Elvis pompadour complete with sideburns. He had a large cigar stuffed into the corner of his mouth, and pale, greasy skin.

His large black eyes narrowed in on mine. "What's yer taste today, madam?"

31

"House Special. Rare."

He led me past the bar to a locked door and, as he fumbled for his keys, the barmaid came over. Her face was tired, older than it probably was. She stopped beside me and fixed me with those sad eyes.

"You fuckin' pig!" she said. "I hope it fuckin' chokes you."

"Git, Susan! Git on back to work and leave her be!"

She cast one last glare at me as she walked away.

"Never mind my sister there. She ain't right in the head now." Then almost whispering, "It's one o' them hormonal things. She just had a baby." He pushed a well-worn key into the old lock and began to work it around, trying to catch the stubborn tumbler.

Sulking, Susan gathered dirty dishes from the emptying tables. She was followed closely by Billy, who watched her from behind, with a slobbering, lusty grin.

Behind me, John made a triumphant grunting noise as the key turned with a click and he pushed the door open to reveal the darkened room beyond. "Your table's a-waitin'," he said, ushering me into the unused room.

He stepped in after me, shutting and locking the door behind us. Sealing us in the tomb-like darkness. Then the light came back, cast from an ornate wagon-wheel chandelier that hung from the ceiling.

This private room was as plain as the saloon bar. There was a single table paired with a single high-backed chair and a door that led into the kitchen area. No windows or adornments drew the eye away from the table.

I took my seat and John disappeared into his kitchen.

I waited in that silent, lonely room for perhaps an hour, but in my anticipation it seemed like years. My mouth began to water. I didn't expect my meal to taste good. Many exotic meats do not taste good to me. My mouth watered in anticipation of the experience, not the taste. I collected rare meats in the same way other women collect jewellery or shoes or handbags.

John, dressed in clean new chef-whites, brought my

32

plate to me on a large silver platter, set it before me, and after wishing me a pleasant meal left me alone to eat.

* * * * *

They were the choicest of cuts, smaller portions than I expected, but prepared skilfully. Six smallish fillets perfectly spiced and roasted to a fine golden hue. Next to the meat was a lemon wedge and parsley garnish. Next to my plate was a crystal flute of champagne.

The meat was exquisite. Never before had I enjoyed such a tender and juicy cut, with a taste that defies definition. I was in heaven. It was so fresh that I could almost hear it cry out as I cut into it. Never had I eaten a meal so slowly, so languidly. I took the smallest of bites, chewing each obsessively until every bit of flavour was milked from it. I ignored the champagne – it would only dull the experience.

Finally the last bite was gone from a meal that I would never forget, and an experience that I would never duplicate. I was satisfied. No sooner had I laid my fork to rest on the plate, when John appeared.

"How was your meal? Satisfactory?"

"Yes' I said with a smile. 'It was perfect."

"Another satisfied customer," he said, scooping up the platter with one pudgy hand and setting a small tray before me with the other. One the tray were three items – the bill, a photo, and an after-dinner mint.

I looked and instantly felt ill. It was not the bill – the high price had been settled on beforehand and was no surprise.

It was the photo.

A small child, an infant really, lay naked on a large cutting board.

All in Working Order

by Chris Wright

Holding the bandages, the nurse stepped back. I looked at the hands. It was hard to think of them as mine as yet, but there they were. A very obvious and angry red join ran between the familiar flesh of my arms and the transplanted hands now attached to them. It felt wrong.

Cradling Matthew in her other arm, Angela reached out to touch me. "We knew it wouldn't be easy."

"Yes, Mr Burroughs," Dr Frazer added. "Give yourself time to adapt. For now, let's just worry about how well the transplant is taking. Can you feel this?"

He drew a feather against the back of my new left hand. I smiled as I felt a faint touch, and again as he moved to the other hand.

"Yes! I'd almost forgotten what that felt like."

"Excellent. The scans looked positive but we like to know for sure. Now to test your movement. Remember, don't expect too much."

I turned my arms over so my hands were resting palms up and concentrated on my index fingers, willing them to curl upwards. Nothing. I focused harder, letting out a grunt with the effort. The end of the left finger lifted, just a little, followed by the other.

"Well done! It may not seem much but that's all we could hope for so soon... Oh, wow!"

I looked at him and saw he was still looking at my hands. My left index finger was fully curled now.

"But... that wasn't me," I said, staring in faint horror at my finger.

He smiled. "Things are still settling, Mr Burroughs, and it shows it's all in working order. It's time to get you home

34

and into some physiotherapy."

So I was released from hospital, still pretty helpless but gradually able to do more and more, hopeful that the day I would be able to hold Matthew unaided was drawing closer.

Two weeks later, the nightmares began.

In fear, a dark-haired woman recoils from me and runs. I give chase, downstairs, through two rooms and out into a darkened garden. There, cornered, she stares pleadingly at me, mouthing words I cannot hear.

I awoke with a start.

A few days later, the dream returned, and again, until it was every night without fail. Each time it progressed a little further until finally I was grabbing hold of the trembling woman's neck, squeezing the life from her body until she went limp.

I told Angela and Dr Frazer, but both reassured me. It was a sub-conscious rejection of the hands, but physically everything was fine. Perhaps I might benefit from some counselling?

One night the dream was different.

It's dark and I'm standing in the nursery, looking down on Matthew as he sleeps soundly in the cot. A little smile plays across his face as he dreams. I reach down, those large, ugly hands wrapping around his little neck. My whole being orders them to pull away. But I am powerless.

Tears stream down my cheeks as I watch him struggle briefly, trying to cry out. All too quickly, he gives in. Motionless, his eyes stare straight at me.

I sit up. I'm in bed, bathed in sweat. Angela sleeps peacefully beside me.

Uncertain, I get up, hurry to the hallway and stand by the nursery door, afraid to push it open, afraid to see what lies beyond.

Angela's hand clasps my shoulder.

Flinching, I pull away.

"What's wrong?" she asks.

The Vanussians are Coming

by Gordon Adams

"This is a grave moment for the Human Race," said the World Controller, standing up to address his audience. He adopted his most sober tone to address the small room, which was full of his senior aides.

"There is no doubt now: the Vanussians are coming. They intend conflict with Earth. We are tracking a fleet of around ten thousand Vanussian combat spacecraft heading directly towards our Solar System. We have at most four days before they arrive within range. The superior technology of the Vanussians means we will face an awesome display of firepower. Thankfully, we have an even greater power with which to fight them."

"What's that?" asked the Deputy Consul for Eurasia.

"Why, the power of *ideas*!" He smiled and glanced to his right, towards a spotty youth sporting a pink shirt. Sitting alongside the youth was a pretty young woman in a bright yellow dress.

"We will fight the Vanussians through the power of… advertising!" added the World Controller with gusto.

He pointed towards the two young people.

"That is why I have invited along to our meeting today the peerless Mr Slinki and Ms Dinki from the world's leading advertising agency, *Slinki and Dinki Inc*. They have been working on an advertising campaign that will unite the entire world's population as never before against the Vanussians! An easy brief, compared to your usual, eh, Mr Slinki?"

The young man winced.

"OK, let's hear your ideas now. I'm turning this meeting over to Mr Slinki and Ms Dinki."

The World Controller sat down and the young man hesitantly stood up.

"Well, after much deliberation we came up with a number of different ideas, that is to say, different creative treatments," said Mr Slinki.

"Cut to the chase!" shouted the World Controller. "Let's hear the best one!"

"Ah yes, well. It may seem a little left field, if you know what I mean. Everyone here knows the Vanussians' eating habits are not, shall we say, the most *decorous*. The Vanussian habit of eating from the floor, crouched on all fours like animals, has been the subject of much mirth here on Earth."

"We know, we know – get on with it!"

"So we distilled the creative idea of depicting Vanussians as *dogs*, as in this advertising treatment."

All eyes were drawn to the e-wall which now featured a Vanussian crouched on all fours, with a dog's head, feasting on a bowlful of human beings. The voiceover said: *"Don't let your family become his next dinner!"*

"Rubbish! Next idea!" said the WC.

"If we could just persist with this one," said Ms Dinki, leaping to her feet. "This was, I have to say, by far the preferred approach. It was rigorously tested in our focus groups! And it lends itself to a number of creative treatments, such as this one."

The e-wall now displayed a picture of a team of Huskies dragging a sledge across the Arctic snow; a Vanussian with a manic look on his face replaced a human handler on the sledge. The heads of the each of the Husky dogs had been replaced with human heads. The voiceover said: *"Your new working day – the Vanussian way."*

"This is hopeless!" yelled the WC, standing up. It seemed Mr Slinki and Ms Dinki's time in charge of the meeting was about to end.

"We'll never beat the Vanussians with this. Crude depictions of our enemies as animals. So simplistic! As if that kind of crude propaganda would ever work in wartime. Yet it researched well, you say?"

"Yes, everywhere – everywhere in the world. Except in Britain," said Mr Slinki. "It appears they rather *like* dogs there."

"Please don't rush to dismiss this approach," Mr Slinki implored. "Consider this. We have an over-arching creative thrust here for our *entire advertising campaign*. It really is this simple: *Two legs good, four legs bad!*"

The WC stood up, hands on his hips.

"Do you really not have anything better than this?" he demanded. "Maybe something more original?"

"Erm, well – we do have one more idea," said Ms Dinki. "This!"

The e-wall now showed a giant torso of the World Controller himself wearing a stern expression, pointing directly towards the viewer. The voiceover boomed out: *"Citizens of Earth: Your World Needs YOU!"*

"As if THAT would work!" sneered the WC. "Still I do look rather good there, don't I? I see you've used that lovely photo of me from the Geneva Congress. I did rather like that one."

"OK, let's brainstorm," said Mr Slinki, seizing control of the meeting again. He grabbed the light baton and wiped the e-wall clean. "Think hard everyone: what is it that unites the people of this world? What do all human beings like?"

"Chocolate?" ventured one voice.

"Motherhood and apple pie."

"Coca Cola," said another.

"Their own children – though they don't really like everyone else's, do they?" said another.

"Beer!

"A nice glass of wine."

"A lie-in on a Saturday morning."

"Football. Cricket."

"Baseball. Basketball.....well – sport, in general."

Soon the e-wall was covered with writing.

"Great! Wonderful!" said Mr Slinki, "I think we're

really getting somewhere now. Now, what is it that the Vanussians have in common, what is it that they all don't like?"

"Mirrors that show them how ugly they are!" shouted one voice.

"Earth food," said another.

"Being made fun of."

"Yes, social embarrassment. They *hate* being shown up."

"Losing 6-1 in the Inter-World Series."

"WHY, YES, THEN I'VE GOT IT!" shouted Mr Slinki, exultantly. "I do believe we can actually do this! I know now how to unite the people of Earth. If we're lucky this might just stop those evil Vanussians in their tracks!"

* * * * *

Two days later, the viral advertising campaign had been released and everyone on Earth had viewed it through their Ethernet connections. The scenes of unity which followed on Earth were unprecedented. The Governments of the three global superpowers – Eurasia, the North American Alliance and the Isle of Wight – issued a unity statement, pledging to do everything in their power to co-operate and prevent the Vanussians taking control of Earth.

The viral campaign suggested that Vanussians hated sport. It depicted them as hell-bent on stopping anyone on Earth playing or watching sport. The videos displayed Vanussians cutting down rugby goals, bursting footballs, burning baseball bats and smashing Ethernet screens broadcasting the Inter-World Series. The campaign strapline was: *Sore Losers?*

Most importantly of all, it depicted Vanussians' sporting ineptitude. The campaign showed genuine clips of the Vanussians playing baseball and missing the ball or playing football and slipping when they tried to take a penalty. The Vanussians were mercilessly lampooned as the galaxy's most hapless sportsmen.

* * * * *

Three days later, the World Government received an urgent message.

"It's a message from the Vanussians, sir," said the WC's top aide. "It is marked *Strictly Confidential* – for your eyes only."

"Send it here," commanded the WC. A few seconds later, he opened up the link on his viewer. He read the message with great interest.

"Well, well, well!" he exclaimed. "It seems the Vanussians have stopped their invasion of Earth in its tracks. Instead, they've challenged us to a game of football next Saturday!"

We Shall Go on to the End

by Chris Wright

Marco handed the speech to the Secretary General.

"Good luck, sir."

Perez took the papers. "Luck is something we so desperately need – but I fear it has deserted us."

The strains of the past days weighed heavily upon him. The man standing before Marco was one barely recognisable from the confident, bullish leader of the United Nations of only a few weeks ago. The detection of the alien spaceships orbiting the Moon; the ultimatum to surrender or face destruction; the efforts to marshal world leaders into a coherent response – they had all taken their toll. Marco could not be sure if there really was more grey in Perez's black hair or whether his demeanour accentuated what had already been there.

"Have courage, sir. The world needs you to be steadfast."

Perez managed a smile, placing a hand on Marco's shoulder. "I will do what needs to be done. I thank you for your support. You have been a great source of strength for many months, but particularly these last few days."

Perez drew himself up, a glint of resolve showing in his eye, spreading to encompass the expression on his face. In a moment, he was transformed.

Marco followed as the Secretary General strode into the adjoining room, from where the broadcast would be made. The camera crew adjusted focus as Perez sat at the mahogany desk. An awkward silence fell on the room. All in attendance, from ambassadors down to staff members such as himself, watched the clock slowly count down the final minute.

41

"Peoples of all nations," Perez said, "for too long we have stood against each other, embroiled in squabbles that emphasised our differences. If these past days have had any positive outcome, it is that they have reminded us of our many and overriding reasons for unity.

"We face a challenge unlike any other, against a species of which we previously had no concept. They come uninvited to Earth and lay an ultimatum before us: Surrender or face the consequences. We do not know them and whatever cruelty motivates them, but neither do they know us. They do not know our capabilities, our resolve.

"For the past days our world leaders and military advisors have been coming together to prepare us for what will come... "

Marco listened intently as Perez spoke, following in his own copy of the speech. He glanced around the room at those privileged to hear the speech directly. They were mesmerised, hoping to hear words of comfort and salvation.

Around the globe, as the broadcast was translated into hundreds of languages, an audience of billions was watching equally intently, craving certainty, a guarantee that everything would be all right. It was Perez's task to give that guarantee, and Marco did not envy him this burden. Even the most expert of assessments were based on little more than conjecture. In truth, nobody knew whether Earth could withstand an assault from the aliens.

"... are hopeful that we can meet this threat ..." Perez continued.

Marco looked to the Secretary General then back down to the speech. *"Hopeful"*? He scanned down the typewritten words. Our generals are *confident*, not hopeful.

He looked to Perez again. Had he imagined it, or was Perez going off script? Glancing around the room, other worried faces met his, their eyes questioning him intently. Marco shook his head and shrugged in response.

What was Perez doing?

"Be assured," the Secretary General continued, "that

your leaders and armed forces will do everything within their power to preserve our species. But we must be realistic and I advise you to seek peace within yourselves or with whichever God you worship."

Panicking, Marco looked around.

Perez had abandoned the script completely.

It lay on the desk now, unread, as he looked directly at the camera. A murmur grew around the room, loud enough to be picked up by the microphones.

He tried to catch Perez's eye, pointing at the copy of the speech he was holding. "Get back to the script," he mouthed. For the briefest of moments Perez caught his gaze – still full of resolution.

"These may be our final hours. If so, we must meet them with dignity, as humanity united. May God have mercy upon us all."

He fell silent, met by a matching, stunned silence around the room. He stood and looked to the ambassadors, dignitaries and staff. "I cannot lie to the world. Not at this critical moment."

The room erupted into a cacophony of voices.

"That's precisely what you damn well *had* to do," the US Ambassador bawled.

"We must have an immediate meeting of the Security Council!" the Chinese Ambassador shouted, struggling to be heard.

Perez nodded. "Ten minutes."

He walked to his office, Marco following closely behind, with the rest thronging after them. Once inside, Marco shut the door behind them. Perez sat wearily at his desk.

"Make sure all the Permanent Representatives of the Security Council are aware of the meeting, Marco," he said.

"Yes, sir." Marco moved to go, then paused. "You do realise what you've done, sir? That was supposed to be your Churchill moment."

Perez rubbed his temples. "But at least Churchill

believed there was a chance of victory. We face a wholly different fight. How could I lie so absolutely?"

"Is that truly what you believe, sir?"

"Leave me. I will be out soon."

Perez watched the young assistant depart the room, shoulders slumped. The furore outside intensified as the door opened and shut.

Smiling, he pulled his smartphone from his jacket pocket and tapped the screen to open a channel to the fleet.

"Admiral, the broadcast was a success. The Earthlings' resolve is severely weakened. Proceed with the next stage."

It's Not Easy Being a Superhero

by Jason McClean

It's not everyday that you find out you have a superpower.

Bunsen Burners are powerful little gas torches that you find in science classrooms. They are used to heat liquids and other things as part of experiments.

Adrian thought they smelled a bit. Something horrible enough to make you want to stay away but not enough to make you sick. The nasty smell was added to gas so you could tell if it was leaking.

Today's experiment sounded stupid. But Adrian had learned that normally when they appeared stupid, that was when he was about to be amazed by something. They were going to see if they could make wet paper burn.

Mr Claws told the pupils to take the paper from the beaker filled with water and hold it in the flame of the Bunsen Burner. Adrian carefully picked it out of the water and held it over the flame

It was soaked in water and he didn't expect it to burn.

Steam rose from it. He reckoned if he left it long enough, then it would burn once all the water was evaporated.

Mr Claws then told the pupils to bin the damp paper and pick up the paper soaked in ethanol. As ethanol was a fuel, Adrian expected it to burn. It duly did so. As the flames ignited all around the classroom, there were gasps from his classmates, shrieks of fear and delight.

Adrian's hand was warm. It was uncomfortable, so he crushed the paper until the flames were extinguished.

Adrian was a little ahead of the rest of the class now. They were frantically dropping paper from tongs into sinks, all hissing and steam.

The final sheet of paper was mixed in ethanol and water. The experiment was to see if it would burn or not. He held it over the Bunsen Burner. It lit up immediately, flames starting with a whoosh, surprising him.

That was when Alison screamed. Then a chorus of screams joined in.

Mr Claws jumped up from his desk, "Drop the paper, boy!" he shouted.

Adrian looked round to see who was causing all the fuss.

Britney was staring at him wide-eyed, mouth open, hands pressed against her cheeks. Adrian almost laughed, but then noticed others were gaping at him.

Simon looked as though he was watching open heart surgery. The gory bit with blood pumping.

Michael was cringing, stepping back, eyes fixed not on Adrian, but his hand.

The ethanol and water soaked paper was in full flame in the palm of his hand.

There was silence in the room. All eyes were trained on him.

Mr Claws grabbed his arm. "Drop the paper."

Adrian dropped the paper.

"Your hand," Mr Claws said. "Does it hurt?" Then, quickly, he turned to a group of pupils. "Go and get the first aid kit and be fast about it."

Adrian smiled at Mr Claws. "My hand is fine."

And it was. A little pink, but fine. He flexed it and pulled his arm back.

That was the first time he realised he was different.

That was when he realised he had a superpower.

That was when the trouble started.

* * * * *

The school nurse told Mr Claws that Adrian was fine, no burns at all. Mr Claws was a science teacher. He only believed what he could see. What he had seen didn't add

46

up.

"Did it burn?" he asked. "Did you feel the heat?"

"It was a little warm," said Adrian. "I thought the water must have taken the heat out of the flames."

"Absolutely not," said Mr Claws.

"Well, I'm okay," said Adrian a little lamely. He should have thought before lighting the paper in his hand. It was a daft thing to do. He had lifted warm things before and dropped them automatically. It hadn't happened this time.

Mr Claws fussed some more with the nurse before shaking his head and returning to the class with Adrian.

It was mayhem. Not much work had taken place and as soon as he walked in there was a surge of questions.

"Are you okay?"

"How's your hand?"

"Mate, if you need a lift home or to hospital, let me know."

"I'm fine." Adrian smiled.

He held up his unblemished hand and his mates crowded round, staring, examining, touching.

High fives followed. The remaining ten minutes of class passed in a blur and then it was break time.

When Adrian got to the canteen, he ordered fish and chips and sat with Bill, his best friend.

"How did you do that?" asked Bill. "The flames were all over your hand."

"No idea," said Adrian. "I must have got lucky, I guess."

Bill sat back looking at him.

"Adrian?"

He turned around. Gary was there with Britney. "Catch," said Gary, throwing something directly at Adrian.

He caught it and felt the heat in his palm immediately. He absorbed the energy and looked at what was in his hand. It was a sausage, still spitting fat. Why would anyone want him to catch a sausage? He put it on the table and wiped his hand on his napkin.

"Dude, how is your hand not burnt? I needed a glove to hold that. We nuked it properly in the micro," Gary exclaimed.

"It felt okay to me," said Adrian.

A small crowd gathered around. He was the centre of attention and wasn't sure it was good attention. He felt like a caged tiger in the zoo with lots of people looking, pointing and poking at him.

Alan appeared, carrying a mug. "Here, try this."

"What?" asked Adrian.

"It's just boiled, hold your hand out."

"Do you think I'm nuts?" exclaimed Adrian.

"Go on, mate," said Gary. "Just a drop on your skin, see if it burns or not."

"Let's get out of here," Adrian said to Bill. But his friend didn't move.

"Just a drop," suggested Bill. "Your hands haven't burnt before, maybe they won't this time either."

Adrian was caught. He had heard of peer pressure but never really experienced it before. Now his friends were cramming round, egging him on.

And, deep inside, he knew he needed to show he was normal. That they had nothing to wonder about. That he wasn't a freak.

Maybe most importantly, there was nothing for them to be scared about.

"Come on, Adrian," said Britney. "I'll pour the smallest drop on your hand. All you have to do is tell me if it hurts."

"Of course it'll hurt, Britney."

"A drop is all."

Adrian was famous for fifteen minutes and he wasn't liking it one bit. He needed to do this to show he was no different. "I'll pour it."

He took the mug. "I can feel the heat through the mug," he said. "I'm not doing it."

Before he could put the mug down, someone smacked his shoulder and the boiled water splashed out, over his hand and forearm.

He instantly felt the heat and absorbed it. Like a shock absorber in a car, he took the force and sent it out into his whole body.

"You freak!" screamed Britney, pointing at his hand and arm.

His hand and arm looked normal, you couldn't even have argued they were red. There was no mark, just damp skin. Adrian thought a couple of seconds too late that he should have screamed and pretended to be in agony.

"Bill, let's get out of here."

He forced his way out through the throng of excited teenagers. There were looks of sheer puzzlement. Others of wonder and confusion, some of admiration. But by far most of the glances he got were distant. They didn't understand. And no-one likes what they don't understand. One or two sets of eyes were calculating, considering.

He broke through and got out of the canteen and the school as fast as he could. Bill was hot on his heels. It was only when they got well past the school gates that they stopped.

"What the hell, Adrian," said Bill.

That summed up exactly how Adrian felt.

* * * * *

Adrian took the rest of the day off school.

But when he turned up the next day, it was worse because he had disappeared.

Girls smiled at him. Even the good-looking ones.

Boys nodded at him. Even the cool ones.

He was summoned to see Mr Squirm, the Headmaster, who told him off for taking time away from school and causing the teachers to worry.

Adrian nodded when he was expected to.

As he was about to leave, Mr Squirm asked about his hand. He wanted to see it. Adrian showed him and left.

All the other questions came from his friends. How did

he do it? Could he do it again? What else could he do?

His Facebook account never had so many friend requests. He went from 15 to more than 500 followers on Twitter.

"Quite the celebrity, aren't we?" said Bill after English class.

"I didn't ask for this."

"No, but you're lapping it up."

"I'm not," protested Adrian. "I hate it. I want to go back to being treated normally."

Bill looked at him. "We need to see if you can do it again."

"I am not a dancing bear at the circus."

"No, but if you can resist heat like that, then you are something... a little special," considered Bill, choosing his words carefully. "Let's go to mine after school and we'll try a couple of experiments."

Although Adrian dreaded the thought of experimenting, it also fascinated him, He had not felt any pain from the boiling water. Maybe he really was special. He wished he were Spiderman. Imagine being that strong, that agile? He'd boss the football team around and never be bullied again.

He'd keep it a secret of course. He'd be subtle about it. While he might have the strength of ten men, he'd only be a little bit stronger than the strongest tackler on the pitch. No-one would ever suspect.

He spent the rest of the afternoon in daydreams, imagining if he were a superhero, before going around to Bill's.

"Right," said Bill. "Hold your hand over the sink. Roll your sleeve up so it doesn't get wet."

"I'm not sure about this," stuttered Adrian, backing away from the steaming kettle.

"I'll only put a few drops on your hand, if it hurts, then I'll stop."

Adrian nodded.

Bill tilted the kettle and a small stream of near boiling

water dropped on to Adrian's hand. He pulled away automatically.

But there was no pain. Only the faint sensation of heat that he automatically absorbed. In fact, he felt better than before.

Bill raised an eyebrow.

"Some more," said Adrian, putting out his arm.

Bill poured more on his hand, up his wrist, steam billowing in the air. The sensation of heat was distant and Adrian absorbed it. He felt stronger. Better than ever. He wanted to shout with joy.

"Man, this is so weird," said Bill. He touched the edge of the kettle and snatched his fingers away, blowing on them.

"I feel great," shouted Adrian, exultant.

Bill's eyes flashed with admiration, then wonder, finally settling on fear.

* * * * *

A week later and life was not so great for Adrian.

Bill was avoiding him. The fear had taken root, Adrian could see it in his friend. People didn't like what they couldn't understand.

The good-looking girls still smiled at him but recoiled at the same time. They admired him – or at least something about him.

Adrian had never been blessed with lots of friends and now he found himself sitting alone in class. Going to the library by himself at lunch time. Praying for the day to end so he could go home. But, once there, it was a nightmare trying to avoid his parents' polite questions about where his friends were. Was he going out to play? How was Bill?

Adrian told them Bill had a girlfriend and wasn't around much anymore. They nodded at that.

He looked forward to football practice on a Wednesday night and the Saturday morning match. His friends there did not know what had happened at school. It was a club team that his Dad had introduced him to years ago.

Adrian was a midfielder. It sort of fitted his life. He didn't stand out from the crowd. He wasn't the natural goal scorer or brilliant defender. He was a bit of everything. He enjoyed it and always took a shot if it came his way. He was good, but already knew he was never going to be a professional.

Saturday's match was against the county's biggest team. They were leading the local league and Adrian always liked starting as an underdog. His team were expected to lose, so if they drew or won it would be a great feeling.

He took to the pitch in determined mood. Average size and weight, he was a bit smaller than most of the other players, but he was up for a battle after the week he'd had at school.

His first tackle had a large boy bounding into him. He was not stopping and Adrian was going to be bowled over. But it didn't happen like that.

Adrian stood firm and waited to be flattened. The boy collided with him and Adrian absorbed the energy. Instead of it smashing him out of the way, it flowed into him and gave him extra strength.

The large boy rebounded off him as if he had hit a wall.

Adrian didn't think, he controlled the ball with his left foot and dribbled forward. He was outside the box. He'd never scored from this far out before. He took aim at the distant goal and let fly.

The ball shot through the air, as if kicked by a professional striker. It was still rising on fierce energy as it shot by the goalkeeper and buried itself in the back of the net.

Adrian couldn't believe it.

Nor could anyone else.

There were no cheers or applause. All the players from both teams were staring at him like he had grown a second head.

The referee blew his whistle and it startled Adrian. The

goal was given. The boy who had collided with Adrian was substituted.

Adrian kept a low profile for the rest of the game. He was exhilarated. He felt like he could easily score again but something inside told him to hold back. Because he could do it didn't mean he should do it.

They won the game. Adrian's goal was the only score. His team were happy and they high-fived him, but at a respectful distance. As though they were worried he might hurt them. He was a tiger in a cage again.

The following week he was picked for the side again and made sure he didn't score. He still played well, much better than usual. Every time someone tackled him, he grew with energy and strength. He could have bulldozed down a wall of players, but he held back, passed with control and in the end his friends celebrated winning with him as though he were on the same side of the cage as they were.

But he knew in his heart he was the tiger that was out of the cage amongst the visitors. All he was doing was hiding his teeth.

* * * * *

When Adrian hid his teeth, he found that life returned to normal.

One morning going to school, he waited for Bill on the walk into class and made a show of tripping and falling in front of him. He sat down hard and held his ankle, grimacing.

"You all right, mate?"

Adrian pretended he hadn't seen him. "Fell over, hurt my ankle, might have twisted it."

"Let's see."

Adrian showed his unblemished ankle to his friend.

"Bit swollen if you ask me," Bill said. "Take it easy. Here, let me help you up."

And that was life back to normal.

53

When the good-looking girls saw him limping, and he thought he put on a rather good show, they stopped taking interest in him.

When Mr Claws told him to put on goggles and fireproof gloves when they approached the Bunsen Burners, he did. And he made sure everyone heard him say how hot his hands seemed.

And he went further. At football practice, one of the bigger lads shoulder charged him. Adrian went down like he had his legs cut from under him. He stayed down, rolled around like they did in the Premiership and asked the coach if he could take a break, he didn't feel well.

Equilibrium restored. Life reset. He was back in his normal position in the hierarchy. Where he wanted to be.

Then he had to make a life or death decision.

* * * * *

Sally was a small kid, only started at school, well known for her love of running everywhere. She was always being told off by the teachers for banging into other children in the corridor.

Adrian's walk to school took him past her house. He instinctively liked her. He liked her sheer joy in moving. Everything in life looked like fun to her.

Adrian walked by her house, didn't see her and walked on. If he was early, she would come running past. If he was late, he might see her on the way home.

This morning he was early.

A couple of minutes after passing her house, she came barrelling past him at full speed. As he was stepping off a kerb to cross a road, her satchel brushed his arm.

A black Range Rover was coming down the road. Maybe 40mph or a little higher, in a 30mph zone.

Clocking it, Adrian stopped.

Sally didn't see it and kept running.

In times of crisis the brain's cognitive functions speed up and that is what gives the impression of time slowing down. Adrian could see things happening in slow motion and needed to make a life or death decision fast. Several of them in fact.

First, did he want to save Sally? An instant answer was yes. Joy like hers was precious, it couldn't be killed, it would be a travesty.

Second, could he grab her?

No, she was moving too fast.

Third, could he shove her out of the way?

Possibly. Probably.

But if he shoved her, then he would risk being hit by the car.

Life or death.

His life or hers?

Adrian leapt into motion before he registered the decision he had made.

His football training helped. He had excellent acceleration and was behind Sally in two bounds. Her smiling face had turned towards the oncoming car and was registering shock. She was directly in front of it, almost within touching distance of her own death.

Adrian shoved her as hard as he could. She catapulted forward. He had used all his momentum to add extra force and was now stranded, standing still. Right in front of the car. No football-honed acceleration was going to help him now.

He had time to look at the driver. The woman's mouth was opening in horror as her foot went from accelerator to brake all too slowly.

Adrian braced himself, calm, ready for death. He had made his decision. He didn't regret it.

The car hit him and he pulled its huge amount of kinetic energy into his body. He didn't know how the Bunsen Burner had not torched him. He didn't know how the boiling water hadn't scalded him. He didn't know how the hard tackle on the football field hadn't felled him. But in each case his body had absorbed the energy.

It happened again.

The front crumple zones of the car did what they were designed to do before hitting the cabin compartment. Then the car pivoted around the immovable object – Adrian. It swung sideways into a parked car, where it eventually settled.

Adrian stood stock still.

Alive.

Engorged with so much energy he wanted to scream. Needed to scream.

He screamed and windows shattered, car alarms went off.

Afterwards, when the accident reconstruction people looked at the scene, they estimated that the car had been travelling at 44mph before the brake was applied. Weighing two and a half tonnes, the force of the impact on Adrian had been enormous. They added that the car crash had also created a sonic boom, damaging nearby property.

Adrian knew better. He had done it. He had to let some of the energy rushing through his body out. He couldn't contain it all.

Straight after the impact, he rushed to see if Sally was okay. She was. Staring up, crying at what had happened.

Adrian thought of the driver and quickly ripped the car door off its hinges and helped the woman out. She was in all sorts of shock, blood running down her face from where the airbag had hit her.

He carried her over to Sally and gently set her down. Energy flowing out of his body and feeling more and more normal with every step.

The police interviewed everyone involved. Sally was fine. A little shaken and given a lesson on how to cross roads. She thought Adrian was a hero.

The driver was fine too. Her nose wasn't broken. Her grasp on reality was a little shaken, though. She couldn't understand how she had not killed Adrian. The police told her a manhole cover had been sticking up and halted the car before she hit him. The damage to the car meant the door had fallen off. Adrenaline in his system was how

Adrian had carried her.

The driver might have bought that story. Probably wanted to buy it and get on with her normal life.

Adrian didn't have that option.

The police had passed him across to men in casual clothing with very serious faces in a big building in central London.

Adrian's family was relocated the next day. London became Newcastle upon Tyne. Their three-bed semi was now a four-bed detached with an acre of land surrounding it. Their ten-year-old car was now a brand new Jaguar. His parents' jobs were terminated and they now worked directly for MI5.

Adrian didn't know what MI5 was but was told they were the good guys.

There were few choices for him. He was carried along at a frantic pace as his whole world turned upside down.

Mr Blue was Adrian's handler. He said, "First day at a new school, you need to be supernormal, as we discussed, do you understand?"

"Yes." Adrian did know. He had a gift. He could absorb energy and then use it afterwards. He was special. He still found calling someone Mr Blue peculiar, though.

"You are very special, Adrian," said Mr Blue. "You can do a lot of good for people. For your country. But right now we need you to be normal. If anyone suspects what you can do, then there will be panic and fear and we don't need that, do we?"

"No."

"I'll pick you up after school and we can start your homework together," Mr Blue smiled. "We are going to turn you into a real life superhero."

Adrian smiled, adjusted his new school uniform and walked to the car.

He had lost friends and a home. His family had lost jobs, social circles and a normal son. The price for saving Sally was high indeed.

Being a superhero wasn't going to be easy.

Flash Fiction 2

By the Light of the Silvery Moon

by Nick Johns

I'd only bitten her, see, not eaten her.

That's why you must always finish your prey. But I was an inexperienced hunter in those days. I had returned to ripping flesh off the old lady when I was attacked from behind.

She knocked me down, eyes flaring red, as wild as anything I ever saw. I rolled and snapped at her heels, brought her down. That's always a good tactic, stops whatever you fight from running off, or from catching you if you run.

So, I got my first good look at her. She was magnificent. A great grey sable with black points, teeth dripping with my blood.

I forgot all about the kill, bit her neck and tried to...

Well, maybe that's a tale for when you've got a bit more fur on your bodies... but as we fought, the full moon set and the change came upon us.

I woke, hungry and hairless, cold as always, and found her waking beside me. As I explained my part in what had happened to her, she attacked me again. But when calmed down, we shared a haunch of her grandma and decided how to explain the carnage.

So, I became the hunter who saved her and fought off the beast. She invented the whole story, even that stupid red cloak...

Hello, dear. Just telling the grand-cubs how we met!

Christmas Spirit

by Nick Johns

"Merry Christmas," I mumbled.

Harried men, clutching last-minute purchases, struck out for home, flowing swiftly past overburdened mothers, dragging weary children from the promise of the few remaining open shops.

Groups of teenagers drifted towards clubs and pubs, an early trickle presaging the flood tide yet to come. Happy huddles of office workers, dishevelled clothing betraying afternoon adventures, weaved down the street − outliers dicing unsteadily with the traffic, proudly sporting traffic cone hats.

The bustling Christmas Eve street appeared awash with humanity. Huddled in the damp cardboard doorway, absently stroking my disreputable mongrel's ears, I knew different.

"Merry Christmas."

Drama

15.07

by Pat Aitcheson

I don't remember when I first saw him, although my life divides into before and after. It's a simple fact that he wasn't there. And then he was. I have a lot of time to think these days, so I might as well write those thoughts down. Maybe it will make sense one day, if not to me then someone else. Nobody believed me then, but it's still true. I'm so very sorry.

He was around four, or so I thought. I found out later he was nearly five, about to go to school that September. I can see him now. He had a mop of curly brown hair, the kind that aunties would love to ruffle while exclaiming how big he'd grown. At first he smiled, showing little white teeth and a mischievous glint in his hazel eyes. He always wore the same green jacket, jeans and black trainers, clutching something in his left hand. I never liked children really, I preferred dogs. Much easier to train and they only

* * * * *

I'm back again, sorry about the sudden stop before. I try to keep track so it doesn't catch me out, but it's hard. I'm torn between watching the clock and trying to ignore it by distracting myself with anything, any mindless activity. There's not much to do here and I can't talk with the others.

Anyway, the first clear memory I have of him, he was in the cereal aisle at Tesco. He looked directly at me and smiled. I guessed his mother was around somewhere and, sure enough, when I glanced back after getting my

Weetabix, he had gone. It should have ended there, there was no reason to remember him. But it didn't end there.

Some days later I saw him again, this time in Waterstones. I thought maybe he was lost, because what was a child doing in the crime section? Still, he wasn't my problem. I turned back to looking through the latest bestseller. Crime fiction is great. People get what's coming to them and all the plot lines tie up. It makes sense, which is so much better than real life.

The boy turned up at the petrol station, across the forecourt near the shop. I had just shut the filler cap. As I walked towards him, he turned and ran behind the building. There was no sign of him when I came out after paying. I asked my mate about it but he was glued to his phone. He hadn't seen him, and after a couple of pints I forgot about it.

* * * * *

It's been a while since my last entry. The tablets make it hard to think straight sometimes, but I need them to sleep. And the insomnia is always worse after my mum visits. I can see the pain in her eyes. But she at least hasn't abandoned me. This visit was different. Mum was trying to understand, she kept asking me why. I told her I couldn't explain it. Just this child, turning up everywhere, haunting my dreams, never speaking, his smile gradually fading.

I couldn't go up to him. What would people say? A grown man and a four-year-old boy? I'm not like that. Although he looked familiar, I thought it was just because I saw him more often. I described him to Mum, and she stared at me, eyes wide. When I mentioned his clothes, she started crying and left without another word. That hurt.

* * * * *

It went on for months. If I was with someone, they never saw the boy. He always vanished before they spotted him.

One Saturday in the shopping centre, I saw him standing silently in the distance while the crowd flowed around him. Something inside me just snapped, and I strode towards him. I was furious and fully intended to give his mother a piece of my mind.

He turned and moved towards the exit. I gave chase, heedless of the strange looks I was getting. It seemed to take forever with people getting in my way. I gave a cry of frustration as he disappeared among the shoppers.

By the time I ran outside, he was nowhere to be found. But he had dropped something. I picked up the red car, still warm from his grasp, and turned it over in my hand. I thought kids only played with consoles these days. I had no energy for shopping after that, and dumped it in the bin. Damned if I was going to give it back.

* * * * *

I'm so tired. Day after day, the same thing. But writing this down helps. A little.

Anyway, after the chase, he appeared every single day. I learned not to mention it to my mates. They said I was obsessed. And I didn't like the looks they were giving me. I'm no paedo – but that boy made it seem like I was a pervert. He stopped smiling. His eyes grew darker. He was accusing me. My anger rose. I was going mad.

My brain fog has lifted since I stopped the tablets. I hide them under my tongue and then store them inside a sock.

One July afternoon, I was driving back from Sunday lunch at Mum's house. I hadn't seen the brat all day, I was starting to relax. Finally, I thought.

But then.

But then, I saw him down side streets and across intersections, standing outside houses and shops. He was everywhere I looked. That's when I knew he couldn't be real. I had to get away. I turned left into my street. Almost home. He stood outside my house, holding up his right hand. I couldn't believe it.

I stamped on the accelerator, shouting, "You're not real!"

I hit him. Even as I braked, tears pouring down my face, he cartwheeled through the air and landed twenty feet away. I wrenched my door open and ran over to his all too solid body, limbs twisted like a discarded ragdoll. By his left hand lay a crumpled red car. Blood covered his shattered head. Black eyes stared right at me. He wasn't supposed to be real.

I can't write any more. Not today. It's time.

* * * * *

I woke up in hospital, handcuffed to the bed, with a policeman by my side. They said I screamed and then blacked out at the scene. I pleaded guilty, of course. Witnesses heard and saw my car speeding towards that poor boy. I didn't get to know his name. Even with DNA they never identified him.

I cried at the trial. They said it showed remorse but I knew better. I was convicted of vehicular manslaughter. They sent me to hospital instead of prison because of the delusions. My mates testified that I was fixated on a child nobody else could see. They never visited.

My mum hasn't come back. Instead, she sent me an old photo, creased and faded. A smiling, curly-haired little boy in a green jacket, jeans and black trainers holds his red car out towards the camera. The back of the photo is stained. I recognise the marks as tearstains. Of all people, I should know what they look like. Her shaky handwriting reads *Jack aged 4½, died in a hit and run, 15.07.83.* Mum looks so much younger then, holding her son tight and smiling. She looks happy. I suppose that's why she couldn't talk about the older brother I never knew.

* * * * *

Now I'm truly alone.

I'm saving up my tablets to celebrate the anniversary. I find I am mostly calm. I don't sleep much. But Jack haunts my days, not my nights. Every day, I cry. Every day, no matter what I'm doing, I burst into tears at 15.07, the precise time I killed him. No amount of meds, no amount of counselling can stop my tears.

I am ready to give my life for what I did. I do not fear dying.

What keeps me awake at night, though, is this; is he waiting for me on the other side, for all eternity?

She Will See You Now

by Allan Shipham

All I could do was think about how uncomfortable I was. I wondered how much more uncomfortable the man wearing the starched clothes was when he told me, "*She will see you now*". I wondered if he has a family and what he told them when he went home. I took a slow, deep breath.

I looked around the room, not sure if I was being watched. The room was large and the furniture out of place, it reminded me of a dolls house. I stared at an extraordinary chest of drawers. If I owned it, I couldn't even fit it in my house. On it sat a lonely mantle clock resting on a lace doily. The clock's face was gold and sparkled and I jumped when Westminster chimes announced the time. I felt for the interview letter in my inside pocket, just in case I had to present it. I raised my clenched fist to knock, but wasn't sure if I was supposed to. I reminded myself to keep breathing slowly and deeply and took another breath.

Do I barge in? Will I be welcomed or scorned? There isn't always a guide when you do something like this. I suppose everyone expects you to know what to do and you do it. As the morning clouds revealed the sun, its rays illuminated my shoes. I wondered how I ever came to be on this threshold. Why was I picked out of all the people who it could've been? Why me? Listening for any noises from the other room, I lowered my hand, reluctant to disturb the silence. I needed another breath.

I noticed a smell I hadn't noticed before, linseed oil or some kind of wax. The floors were shiny. Maybe it was floor polish. There was also a hint of apples in the air. I couldn't see any, so I wondered if there was one of those discreet fresheners. I dismissed such a silly thought. The aroma reminded me of a field where I used to live, the smell of the pine trees and the freshness of the flora. The shimmer of the sun off the polished floor was like the glint off a stream nearby. How far away it was from me right now. I took yet another mouthful of air.

I decided to bite my teeth, open the door and walk in. I reached out and grabbed the doorknob. I didn't turn it, I needed to compose myself. The brass knob felt hot and sticky to my hand. I had to make a move soon, I was summoned. Was I holding her up from doing something more important? I paused. I felt the weight of my wallet and jingled my car keys… they were still there. I'd already put my phone on silent, that was in my trouser pocket. I had everything I came with. The rest was up to me. I could feel my heart starting to race. I wanted it to stop, so I released the handle. I drew a shallow gasp of air.

I looked at the clock again. A couple of minutes had passed. It felt like hours. If I walked in now, would she accuse me of being late? I knew it should just knock and enter, but something was holding me back. Maybe I wasn't good enough? Maybe there was someone better than me? *What was wrong with me?*

I looked down at the floor. My shoes were shiny, just like the last time I checked. I felt sick to my stomach. That egg cress roll might not have been the best choice. I rushed my fingers through my hair. Some gel stuck to my hand, the same hand I was going to offer in a handshake. I rubbed it across the backside of my trousers. I had to move on, and my path was through that door. I raised my hand again, rapped the door, turned the knob clockwise and moved forward into the room.

I fell to the floor like a sack of potatoes. In the confused moments after, I remember telling myself… to breathe.

Apart from the Smell, of course

by Beth Heywood

The basement was dimly lit by a single bulb, suspended from the ceiling. Roger looked around. There wasn't a spec of dust anywhere. Good. That was how he liked things to be. Clean, neat and tidy and all was right with the world. Right now he needed to think and this was his sanctuary, his haven. He walked to the cabinet in the corner, took out a glass and poured himself a generous shot of scotch. Then he walked over to the table, sat at the armchair behind it, took a sip of his drink and looked at his options.

He thought about his suppliers. They were safe. He had made no written record of them anywhere. That was kept carefully filed away inside his head. They were safe, so if the worst case scenario eventuated, there could be no reprisals. Ever.

Then there were the individuals who cleaned the cats. They, too, were safe. Besides, there was only a handful of cat cleaners working at any given time. Of course, it was a specialist job, each cat requiring a different kind of cleaning to the rest. Much work was involved. Testing for lice, tics, disease-carrying fleas, etc etc. It all took time and patience.

After the cat-cleaners came the tanners. They worked at preserving the skins. This was a most important job in the scheme of things, maybe the most important, for without it, nothing else could successfully proceed.

There was the little matter of euthanasia. That, too, was an important job. But it was done, quickly and kindly, in an ante-room of the basement. As the walls were sound-proofed, Roger's wife and family never had any idea of what went on down here. Apart from the smell, of course. But even that lessened with time. It was merely the tanning smell, not exactly the smell of death. Naturally there would be no putrefaction in here.

It had been a well thought-out project, Roger reflected. Had it really all originated from himself? Well, yes, he had to admit that it had. In truth, it was a labour of love. He rose from his seat and walked among his cats. He loved them all but he loved their future owner even more. It was for her he was making all these sacrifices.

Of course, he knew exactly which cat would suit her. And no, it wouldn't be just one cat. For example, take the largest one, a species of tiger. For Roger's needs he would require two. Or from a smaller cat, maybe a dozen. Each cat had to be turned into several matching products for his love. She always liked to be well-dressed which was one of the things he loved about her.

Roger looked around him. Tigers, lion, leopard, snow leopard, panther, the list went on. But finally, his prize, and hers: ocelot. That would make her a coat, matching hat, gloves, muff, handbag, and shoes. Yes, it would take a lot of skins. But it would be worth it.

Roger drained his glass, walked across the basement to the fur-sewing machine and made a start.

All My Sins Remembered

by Nick Johns

"I've watched through his eyes, I've listened through his ears, and I tell you he's the one."

"He says not. And he has witnesses."

Still returning to my mind from his, I peel off the electrodes.

"Well, they all say that. And his kind of money can always buy witnesses."

"His kind of money can buy us trouble." Her voice was shrill, like a recorder blown too hard.

I peer at the man, no, the animal, restrained in the machine.

"Relax. He's the one. I'm certain. The question is, what do we do about it?"

"We could go to the police... " Her words falter.

"Money," I counter, and watch her eyes drift, unwilling, back to the machine. "Anyway, what would we say about how he came to be here, hooked into that?"

"What then?"

"It's up to us. No. It's up to you. She was your sister."

She twirls her hair around an absent-minded finger.

"You're sure? No mistake? No doubt?"

"I saw it all," I mutter, not meeting her eye.

The man in the machine groans and opens bleary, confused eyes. They swiftly regain focus, a gleam of predatory recognition lighting in them, and they burn into her back.

Her shoulders rise as she takes a breath.

"Then do it," she whispers.

"Me? You don't want to...?"

"No! Please. Just do it... for me."

I turn and press the button.

His body convulses. His eyes screw tight, mouth a rictus grin, teeth biting into lower lip, blood trickling down his chin. A low, bestial howl escapes clenched jaws and his back arches, rigid, straining at the restraints. With a final whimper, he falls back, limp.

She stands, transfixed and shaking, barely audible sobs hissing past clenched teeth.

I reach to stroke her hair, breaking the suffocating silence.

She jerks her head away.

"There, there," I croon to her, "it's done. Go now." My gentle push propels her toward the door and her own solemn momentum carries her through it.

I turn back to the machine, powering down the humming apparatus, consigning it, with a flick of a final switch, to its own little mechanical death.

A deep, shuddering breath and a blood-bubbled cough erupts from the body in the machine.

I move to stand before him, directly in his eye line as his lids flicker open.

I hold his incurious, passive gaze for a moment, searching.

No-one, not even I, could be certain of everything that running the machine at such intensity could do to a mind.

Certainly an absence of memory. He will never remember anything of his life. But beyond that?

His innocent storm-grey eyes look back into mine, unblinking and I see the absence of... of what? Intelligence? Consciousness? Identity?

I busy myself, polishing shiny surfaces for any final tattle-tale marks that might betray us, then leave the laboratory.

Amid the concrete echoes of the empty car park, the shakes hit me. I slump against a pillar, its cold, rough surface pitting my forehead.

I dig shaking nails into the palms of my hands, chasing pain to replace the still fresh images the machine and I had retrieved from his mind. I dig for the cleansing blood below the skin, seeking absolution for thoughts that were now mine alone.

I had, as I'd told her, watched through his eyes and listened through his ears, but what I had not told her, since I had sifted through his memories, I now remember every one of them.

Would time fade them, wash them away like a painting left out in the rain or, as the new owner of those vile memories, am I somehow now culpable?

I push off the pillar, stand straight, shake my head and blink away the thought.

She does not need to know.

The Nights are always the Worst

by Deborah Bromley

Bella wipes the counter top and reaches for the paper towel to dry it. For the second time. She steps away and checks each part of the kitchen. Cooker, gleaming. Fridge doors, polished. Floor, spotless. Back door, double locked and blind pulled down. Front door, locked, key in the lock and security chain in place. She hesitates, then turns the kettle on to make a bedtime drink. Her hand trembles as she pours the boiling water into the mug.

Upstairs in the bedroom, the curtains are already drawn, the bed turned back, revealing smooth white sheets and comfy pillows. Pale yellow light pools around the bedside, inviting her to slide beneath the covers. Max's side of the bed is empty and unlit. Max's side is... Don't look at his side, idiot! He's only away for one night! That's right. Just one little night. Take a deep breath now. Take your pill. Drink the damn drink. Stop thinking about it. Nothing will happen.

If only Max could be here right now to tell her: "I promise you, Bella. Nothing will happen. It will be just the same as normal, except for no snoring from my side. There. You smiled! I knew you could. But if you think it's too soon after... just tell me. I can easily change my plans."

* * * * *

Darkness has its own way of shaping a room. She knows the bedroom landscape off by heart. The sliver of light under the door. Reflecting off the thick drapes with their pretty golden lustre. The shadow where the armchair

77

squats in the corner. The pattern on the ceiling from the lampshade. That stupid lampshade she'd wanted with the feathers dangling around it.

Deeper and deeper she slides into the darkness. The bed is soft. She feels weightless; sleep will come soon. She moves her hand to check, just in case. Yes, I'm safe in my bed. I'm not sleeping, but I will be. Any moment now...

* * * * *

The darkness thickens. Her eyes adjust. It's later. And she's awake. Bed, check. Shadow of the armchair, check. Now she has to concentrate like she's been taught: "Breathe, breathe. Close your eyes and count to ten. When you open them you'll feel calm and relaxed."

It isn't working.

Sweet Max. His voice is there in her head: "Bella, Bella. Darling. You can do it, I know you can. Remember how strong you are, my fearless, feisty lady. Your confidence will come back to you, baby. I swear. One step at a time."

Then the feeling comes over her. Pressing down hard on her chest. The weight is on her chest. She has to sit up right this minute.

Bella gasps. Once, twice, three times for luck. And shakes her head. She sits up in bed and calms herself down. It's fine. She wasn't awake at all. It was just a half-sleeping kind of dream. The worst kind. Snippets of fake reality playing like movies in her head. Imagined hands pushing her down into the bed. So real at the time, but they soon fade when you wake. She'll be fine in a minute. Well, not totally fine. As if that could ever happen.

The next thing she knows there's a chink of light between the curtains. The bedside clock reads 4.45. Her head relaxes into the pillow. It's almost over. Tentative birdsong outside her window. A tiny flutter of hope blooms inside her. There's only an hour or so to wait before it's okay to get up. Maybe she's done it. Maybe Max is right. One step at a time. That's all it takes. She wonders if it's safe to take a hopeful peek out of the window. Soon there'll be a sunrise.

The thick curtains feel strangely languid in her hands. The whiteness of her arms gleams in the dark as she pulls them apart. Grey dawn light has emptied the garden of form and familiarity. There is no sunrise yet and it's too late, much too late to cover her eyes. Her arms dangle uselessly by her side. Because there he is again. The black shadow outlined against the bleak morning light. He looks up into her face, as she knows he will. He always does. His hollow face and empty eyes. The man she killed. Wet road. Can't see the road. Brake now. Brake, you idiot. Too late. Always too late.

Dad

by Beth Heywood

It was two weeks since Mum had died. We'd all loved her, albeit in different ways. Johnny and I had loved the cuddles and hugs, the wide smile on her face as we came inside from a whole day of playing out, and she had tea waiting for us.

Dad said he loved her for her mind and her soft, soft skin.

Since she'd died suddenly of a heart attack, I, at the age of ten, had to become the woman of the family and seven-year-old Johnny needed comforting. I was doing that. Dad seemed incapable of offering any comfort to either of us.

So I did the best I could, as Mum would have wanted. I didn't know if it was enough.

I cooked for all of us, as Dad said he didn't know how to. The only culinary advice Mum had given me before she died was, "Mince, sausages, and chops, they're the cheapest meats. Add potatoes and green vegetables and you've got a meal." That was the only domestic science lesson I ever had. Dad never complained about my cooking, which was just as well for both of us.

But he had a formidable temper. It certainly frightened me but Johnny stood up to him. He would shout, raise his fists, his face becoming diffused with blood, his eyes wide and staring till it looked as if he'd burst.

Mum used to get upset with me and Johnny when Dad lost his temper with us. She was convinced it was always our fault. "If you're not careful, he'll have a stroke and die," she'd say, "and if he dies, we'll have no money coming in and what will we do then?"

But today was different. She couldn't blame us any

more.

Johnny was sitting up in bed. His bed was small and narrow. To the left of him was an alcove. To his right was a chest of drawers, then a door leading to a staircase going down to the next level. I stood at the foot of the bed, leaning against the wall. We often talked at bedtime.

"Elizabeth!" shouted Dad from downstairs. "Come down and do the washing up!"

I rolled my eyes. "Please" and "thank you" were words that never fell out of my Dad's mouth. Besides, I'd done all the cleaning and all the cooking. Why couldn't he wash up for once?

Johnny giggled. "Sooner you than me,"

At that moment, the bedroom door swung open.

"What did you say?" Dad yelled.

"Nothing."

"WHAT DID YOU SAY?"

"Sorry."

"Stay there!"

I knew no good would come of this. Why the hell couldn't Dad just settle down and act normal?

Within seconds, he returned to the bedroom. In his hand was the thickest of his canes.

I watched in horror as Johnny tried to get out of bed. He got as far as the alcove. Dad raised the cane and brought it down on Johnny's backside. It sounded like something hard and heavy hitting the bulky arm of a leather chair. I waited for Johnny to scream but he didn't. He always had been a brave little boy.

Quick as a flash, another blow. Johnny stumbled into the wall. He didn't fall. He didn't scream.

I could hear my heart thudding fast, I tried to breathe slowly. I could feel sweat running down my forehead, into my eyes, down my cheeks, off my chin. A hot stream of pee ran down my legs.

Down came the cane again.

"That's enough, Dad," I cried. "You'll break his tail-bone. You'll kill him!"

Johnny turned around, his eyes blazing, his face ashen. He caught the cane as it came down yet again. He pulled it one way. Dad pulled it the other. Dad won and dropped it on the floor. I approached him and picked up the cane.

Dad was shaking with rage, his face red with anger. I remembered Mum's warning about giving Dad a stroke.

How could she have left me with this mess to sort out?

Chasing the Horizon

by Pat Aitcheson

Xander watched the bacon bits sizzling in the pan and sighed. He had to cut off the mouldy parts, since there was little else in the fridge. If he didn't sell a painting soon, he'd be on the street. It had all been so different years ago, when Xander Le Fevre was the toast of the art world.

He specialised in disturbing dreamscapes that owed a debt to Dali but were more fantastical. Monstrous creatures roamed his canvases and critics loved his "glimpse into the eerie world of the grotesque", as *The Times* put it.

These days, he sold hardly anything. The world had moved on and it was harder to surprise the modern generation.

The ketchup bottle was almost empty, too. He squeezed the last few drops on to a slice of stale bread. He spread it out in a pleasing pattern with his finger, thinking it looked like an ancient sign of some kind.

"Hmm, what was it he said on *Demon Hunter*? Something like *congregandum eos coram me?* Not that you can believe a TV programme.*"*

He turned to get the bacon and almost screamed at the apparition in the corner.

"No, you're not going mad, yes, I am real, yes, you did summon me. By accident, apparently." The creature spoke with a weary inflection. It folded its huge, leathery black wings with a dry, rustling sound.

Xander backed away clutching his chest, sandwich forgotten. "What the hell? How did you – "

"Okay, look," the creature snapped, "I don't have time to waste here. You traced my summoning mark upon the

83

food offering, and I am bound to grant you a single wish. Usual rules. No wishing for wishes, no wish that affects another person, blah blah. I'm sure you know how this works."

Xander swallowed. "Fine. And payment? I'm not stupid."

"Of course not, dear boy. I'll take that delicious smelling bacon sandwich when you've finished making it."

Xander examined the demon. Its head brushed the ceiling and it held flaming swords in the upper pair of its four arms. White hair flowed around its goat-like face while smoke trailed from a mouth armed with rows of shark-like teeth. A single horn curved back from its high forehead. The body was vaguely humanoid but immensely muscular and in the centre of the abdomen a red orb slowly pulsed.

The most unusual thing was the absence of eyes. Where Xander expected red pupils, instead a black void hovered under the forehead like a blindfold. Heat scorched his skin. This was a hundred times better than anything he had ever dreamed up.

"Come on, get on with it." The demon thrust one sword forward for emphasis.

Xander flinched but held his ground. "Sorry, you are most wondrous, er, sir, and I am just admiring your fearsome appearance."

"Whatever you say," the demon growled. "You have but one minute more. Wish, or it will go ill with you."

Xander was stumped. What did he want? What? Not immortality or riches beyond the dreams of avarice, there was always a catch. His eye landed on the canvases and half-finished works stacked around the studio. Yes, this he could do.

"I want to be able to sell my work for millions of pounds, so I can enjoy my life on my own terms."

"I don't hear a wish in there. You must be," the demon chuckled, "specific."

Xander took a deep breath. "I wish for the skill of perfect execution."

The demon tilted its head. "What will that profit you?"

"My imagination is great and my works will be astounding. I will name my price." He finished the sandwich and presented it to the demon. "Thank you, sir."

"It is done." The demon vanished. All that remained was a sulphurous smell and two black scorch marks on the ceiling.

Xander rubbed his eyes. Did that really happen? Maybe it was a dream. But the sandwich was gone. He made some toast, and wondered.

* * * * *

In the middle of the night, he sat bolt upright. He knew what to paint. He ran downstairs, set up a new canvas and got to work.

A few days later there was a knock at the door. Xander was loath to stop, he was on a roll, but the knocking continued. He snatched the door open.

"I'm working, Fabian," he yelled and went back inside.

Fabian strolled in, elegant in a deep green velvet suit and polished black boots. "That's good, because otherwise I'd have to ask for the advance back. My little gallery can't afford – what's that?"

Xander continued to paint. "Just something from my imagination."

"It's very striking. How long until it's finished?"

"I don't know, but longer if you don't leave me alone."

"Okay, okay. I'll pop back next week."

A week later, Fabian returned. "Xander, this is your best work for ages."

Xander didn't look away from his canvas. "You can't have it."

"What do you mean? You owe me! Did you get a better offer? I'll match it."

"I mean it's not ready yet. Come back next week."

Fabian returned many times over the next few weeks, offering larger and larger sums for the painting. He couldn't tear his eyes away from the red and black figure so vividly depicted.

"This just might be the best piece of your entire career." He turned to Xander and frowned. "Are you eating, Xander? You look thin."

"Bring me a sandwich. I have to keep going."

"It looks amazing, please let me show it at the gallery. You can name – "

"I'm close, but it's not perfect yet!" Xander roared.

Fabian backed away. These artistic types had to be handled carefully, especially when they got that mad look.

Xander barred the door and returned to work.

Some weeks later, Fabian had to get the police to break down the door. Xander's emaciated body lay on the floor in front of his easel, brush in hand. The canvas crackled with dark life in red, black and gold, with wings, flames and swords, with hair moving in an unseen wind. Under the brows was emptiness, black but something darker, a presence waiting just out of sight.

The longer Fabian looked at it, the more unsettled he became.

The paramedics averted their eyes as they took the body away.

Fabian remained, staring at the picture, drawn to the void. Trying to see the eyes.

He didn't notice T'rrak the demon standing behind him.

"It's an excellent likeness, he almost captured my eyes." T'rrak chuckled, although no-one heard him. "Almost. Of course, attaining perfection is like chasing the horizon. He needed to let it go."

Widow at the Window

by Allan Shipham

I suppose it all started when I woke up. I had a wash, dressed and had my breakfast. Then, when I walked through the front door to take my Red Setter for a walk, I woke up and realised it was a dream and I had to do it all over again.

Then, there was the incident on the back field, while I was walking the dog. A kid with strawberry blond hair walked across the field on his way to the local secondary school, my dog bolted over to him for a bit of a fuss and frightened the living daylights out of him. I don't think he likes dogs. Anyway, he didn't need to get so aggressive and abusive when, slapping my thigh, I called my dog back. After all, it was my daughter who called the dog Ginger, not me!

Anyhow, I got to work and tried to get on with the rest of my day. Someone refilled the coffee machine with salt instead of sugar and made me heave a few times and nearly lose my breakfast. I stubbed my toe on the photocopier twice, the dodgy strip light over my desk kept flickering on and off again and they're digging up the sewers outside. At times, it was hard to even breathe when someone left the door open.

To cap it all, the boss put everyone in a foul mood after telling us we wouldn't get our bonuses. Fortunately, I was the office hero for about five minutes when I re-checked the spreadsheet and found that Zebra Paints account had fallen off the spreadsheet.

By noon I needed a break so I went for a walk.

It suddenly became very dark. Storm clouds gathered and burst into rain showers of different intensities. By the time I got to the junction where they had opened that new art gallery, I was soaked. Although the rain eased, I needed shelter, a cup of tea and a chance to dry out. I ran into the gallery.

Later, as I turned a corner, I was struck by the bright light and silhouette from a full-length bedroom window. The old thatched house was painted with a soft pink pastel colour. The ground floor was covered with Virginia Creeper and spotted with purple Wisteria that appeared like grapes hanging from a vine. Water in the road reflected bright colours and a mirror image of the house. It was breathtaking. Although it was slightly hazy, I could also see the details of the silhouette.

I sat down on a bench and looked back up at the actual silhouette in the window upstairs. It was the distinct outline of a middle-aged woman sitting on a chair. Quite why she had a light on and why she sat between the light and the open window eluded me. Her dress appeared to be from around the beginning of the last century. As usual, my mind ran away with me, I suspected she was part of an amateur dramatic group or something like that, trying on outfit from a show.

She must've been close to the window as I could see the light shining through her long hair. It lay across her shoulders and flowed over the back of the chair. At first, I thought she was praying as her hands were close to her face. But, after staring for a while, I decided she was teasing her eyes with a handkerchief he'd wrapped around her fingers.

All the time I stared she didn't move. I wondered what on earth could keep someone concentrating that much, completely frozen in time. There was something melancholy about her pose.

I wanted so much to go over, knock on her door and ask if there was anything I could do to help. But I know you can't do that kind of thing. There were no other lights on, so I think she was the only one that was in the house.

I wanted to know how long it would be until someone

came home to keep her company, or indeed if anyone was ever going to come home. It was such a big house for only one person. Surely she should have someone living there, even if it was a lodger.

Then I noticed some birds resting on telephone lines. How long had they been there? Why hadn't noticed them earlier? I couldn't hear any singing, of course, but the poor little things were probably soaked and trying to dry out. Like me.

I looked back up at the window to see if the lady had moved or even noticed me. But no! Seeing her so sad made me sad. Sometimes I have to look at other people's lives to realise how lucky I am and what I have to be grateful for.

"Acrylic."

I turned to see an elderly woman sitting next to me on the bench.

Smiling, she continued, "I love acrylic paintings, don't you? The texture of the paint adds so much to the depth and the experiences of the image. Sometimes it feels like you're really there. And the wisteria – quite lovely!"

She winked, squeezed my hand, got up and wandered off.

Only then did it occur to me to look at the plaque next to the painting.

Widow at the Window – by Deirdre Cameo – 2017.

I was late back to work. Luckily, they'd fixed the coffee machine.

No Turning Back

by Chris Wright

A cold, salt spray peppered the air as the skiff struck a wave. The light from the gas-powered lantern cocooned the vessel, protecting the six men within from the blackness beyond.

"Are you all right, boy?"

Normally, Ghedi would have bristled at being called a boy. He was fifteen years old and no child. The AK47 weighing uncomfortably on his lap was ample evidence, however, that this was no normal time.

He put on as brave a smile as he could and nodded. "Yes, Uncle Assad. I'm fine."

"Remember what I taught you. When we take the ship, don't fire unless you have to." His uncle grinned. "You could hurt somebody with that."

The four other men in the skiff laughed.

Ghedi nodded, but grimaced inwardly. These men, even his uncle, were the sort his father had warned him about – joking about the lives of innocent men as if they were nothing.

Assad was looking at him closely. "What is it, boy?"

"Nothing, Uncle."

Assad leaned forward, grabbing Ghedi's chin with one hand, effortlessly forcing him to look him straight in the eyes.

"Still you have doubts?"

Ghedi said nothing, moving his eyes to break the gaze.

"Your father was naïve." Assad let go, leaned back and gestured out at the sea beyond the skiff. "His high principles didn't stop the foreigners stealing the fish and destroying our livelihoods. When we took action and the fish returned, Erasto condemned us – but he was still willing to accept the benefits of our work. He was a hypocrite."

Ghedi's gaze locked back on to his uncle. "My father was a good man!"

"A good man... Well, look where it got him. Scrabbling around to provide for your mother and your sisters until an early death." Assad's face softened a little. "But you have more sense. You know what you must do to look after them."

"Yes, Uncle."

Ghedi gazed out into the blackness, watching the bobbing lights of the other skiffs travelling nearby. In the east, the first faint hints of dawn were stirring. It would only be an hour or so before they reached the targeted ship. Uncle Assad's arguments made sense, but Ghedi knew what his father would say: that, first of all, a man must do what was right. If he did, then Allah would provide.

That was easier to believe when his father had still been alive and their fishing boat was seaworthy. Now it was his responsibility to feed his family – with a damaged boat and no money to mend it.

The glow in the east grew gradually until the sun lifted above the horizon, bathing the sea in its brightness. He had seen the dawn across the ocean many times but still its beauty was moving.

To the south, the shape of a large container ship grew visible. One of the men in the lead boat signalled and the flotilla spread out into a V-shape and increased their speed so that Ghedi felt a churning in his stomach as his skiff hit the waves more forcefully.

Maybe the churning had nothing to do with the sea.

Ghedi could make out a figure on the deck of the ship, walking slowly, showing no sign that he was aware of the incoming boats.

He glanced at his uncle.

Assad wore a broad smile, his eyes shone with

excitement. "You'll never feel as alive as you will in the next few minutes, boy. Never feel so powerful."

Ghedi nodded, bowed his head and whispered, "I'm sorry, Father."

One trip with his uncle.

Then he could afford to repair the fishing boat and be a good son once more.

Just one trip.

The Wilbur Street Murders

by Allan Shipham

William peered over the fence into the garden of the old man next door. He frowned as an unfamiliar black cat explored the wilderness. The cat traced its way through a safe path as it made its way to the old man's house. A breeze stirred lavender bushes and scented the air, the smell reminded the eight-year-old boy of his grandma's visits. He noticed the cat sniff around a pair of cellar doors. William raised his arm to shield himself from the glints of sunlight reflecting off a padlock looped through the cellar door handles.

A downstairs window creaked open. There were several coughs and splutters from inside.

"I can't establish the cause of death," a deep voice explained. "We'll have to wait for the post mortem. Take a few more pictures, lock the place up and don't forget to turn off the services... "

"Yes, sir!"

"... and don't forget to close that window!"

The rest of the conversation became muffled and William heard doors slam inside the house. He had seen police enter the house. He wanted to know more.

The black cat cried loudly in an almost human voice. William watched as it arched its back and spat at a small cellar window.

"Hiya, William! What's happening?" His school friend Ben pulled upon his bike, loosened his cycling helmet and dropped his bike to the ground.

"Dunno! I think it's old Bert next door!" He glanced around. "I think he's died!"

William gave Ben a hand to step up on a wobbly crate

so he could also look over the fence. William noticed his hand was stained with creosote and wiped it on the side of his shorts. "Watch that cat! I saw six cats go in to Bert's basement yesterday and not one come out. Bit weird. He hates cats!"

"The cat man of Wilbur Street?"

"Nah! I think something bad happened!"

"The wind tastes just like them purple sweets," Ben said. "But I can't see any cats."

William looked back over the fence.

"I just saw one. It was hissing … right by the cellar."

Ben jumped off the crate, looked closely at the sticky substance on his hands and wiped them on a soft leafy plant nearby.

"Let's take a look. We should investigate!"

They pushed back a loose fence panel and entered Larry's garden.

As they made their way to the back of the house, both scratched their shins on the old, woody lavender. Beneath the ground floor window, the boys became aware that someone was looking out. They pressed themselves against the wall. Whoever it was, checked the window was closed and swiftly drew the curtains.

"That was close!" said Ben.

"That's the police!"

"We should go!" Ben exclaimed. "I've changed my mind! My dad'll kill me if the police arrest us."

"Don't be a chicken!" William whispered and shook his head. "Bert's put a padlock on the doors, so we'll have to go in through there." He pointed toward the small window.

Ben looked back up at the closed curtains. They pressed on.

They reached in, unhooked the stay and forced the window open. William went first. After squeezing through, they landed on a cold laminated surface.

"What's that awful smell?" Ben said, pinching his nose. "It's revolting."

"I can hardly breathe!"

"And I can hardly see in this light," said Ben. He coughed and covered his mouth.

Pressing his finger to his lips, William pointed above and stabbed the air a few times.

"I know!" whispered Ben.

"What was that?" a voice bellowed from above.

Both looked up.

Dust sprinkled through the meagre light rays that reached into the room. The boys heard what sounded like feet pacing around and someone try to unlock an internal door at the top of a staircase. They looked at each other in fright.

"Look around, let's hide," hassled William.

As the boys ventured into the darker corners of the room, they became more accustomed to the light. Ben's foot stumbled against a small solid object. He picked it up.

"What's this?"

"Hey, look what I found on this table," said William. "I think it's a toy."

"I've got another one here. There are loads, just lying around." Ben moved back to the centre of the room and held up his new toy. It flopped back, revealing a cat's face.

"Wow, this one's got a name tag. It's called... Tum... ble... down?" He shook his head. "Stupid name for a cat!"

William dropped the toy he was looking at. It made a thud as it hit the floor.

"These are real cats!" He turned to his friend. "And they're all dead!"

"You're shitting me!" Ben cried.

"This one's called Oscar!" He pointed at the one on the floor.

Ben dropped Tumbledown like the time he picked up a hot sausage off the barbeque.

"Ewww! " Ben rubbed his hand across his t-shirt.

As William stepped away from the cat, he knocked over a small metal stepladder sending it crashing like cymbals to the floor. A half-eaten chicken carcass rolled across the floor, before coming to rest in the pool of light. The boys stared at each other as they heard movement and voices above.

"There is someone in the cellar!" a voice shouted.

William could hear his heart beating fast. Frantically the boys climbed back up on the work top and scrambled to get out. As the staircase door eventually opened, a strong beam of light reached into the cellar and panned around.

"Is anyone there?"

The light just missed Ben's trainers as he grabbed William's hand and was pulled to safety.

They rushed across the garden and went back through the fence.

"Get your bike, let's ride around in the street!" William barked.

William and Ben tried to look inconspicuous as they watched from William's front garden. They saw the police carry out some sealed evidence bags, lock the front door and go to their car.

The boys shared a surprised look as a policeman approached them.

"Thank you for leading us to the basement, boys. It looks like you helped solve the case."

"We weren't in any basement!" William muttered.

"And we didn't see those dead cats!" Ben covered his mouth as soon as he realised what he'd said.

The policeman shook his head and smiled. "The old man trapped the cats after they escaped from that cats' home down the road. He gassed them but unfortunately it looks like he was overcome by the gas after he shut it off and he collapsed as well. If you hadn't been poking around, we probably wouldn't have discovered what happened down there for weeks."

The boys stared in silence.

"Seems you two, were really lucky. Gas is heavier than air, but it all escaped by the time you broke in. You do know you could have died in there. I hope you've learned a valuable lesson."

The boys took a sideways glance at each other, then looked down.

"Curiosity killed the cats!" the policeman chuckled.

"Are we in trouble?" Ben said.

"No, I can't prove anything. But why did you go in there in the first place?"

"We wondered what happened to the black cat. It wanted to go into Bert's basement but we knew Bert hated cats!"

When Violet Met Judy

by Michael J Richards

When Mum heard Judy Garland was in town and in her performance had sung "Over the Rainbow," she said, "Ron, that's my favourite song. I'd love to hear her sing it."

That was all I needed. I'd met Judy originally a couple of years before when she first came to London. And after that, whenever she came over, Reg looked after her. She especially liked going around the pubs in the East End. And, of course, everyone loved her. She'd walk in and the piano player would strike up a fanfare, then she'd spend the whole evening singing her heart out. But, by then, she was drinking a lot and taking drugs as well. So, after a while, because I didn't like to see her making an exhibition of herself, I stayed away.

But, in the early part of 1966, when Mum said she'd like to hear Judy sing, I knew I couldn't disappoint her. I got Reg to ask Judy if she'd pay our mum a visit. Reg told me she didn't hesitate. He said he'd drive her to Mum's house in Bethnal Green. 178 Vallance Street, where Mum had lived since 1939.

I went round to Mum's the morning of the day Judy had arranged to visit. I expected her to be fussing around the place, sweeping up and polishing. But there she was, as cool as a cucumber, sitting in her chair, reading the *Daily Express* and drinking a cup of tea.

"Aren't you going to tidy up, Mum?" I said.

"Why should I?" she said. "I go around every day. You're always bringing people back here for your business meetings. Today's no different."

"But what about something to eat?" I said. "She'll want

something to eat."

"Don't you go telling me how to receive a visitor," she snapped.

"No, Mum," I said. "Sorry, Mum."

"She'll get what everyone else gets when they come round."

"Well, aren't you going to get it ready?"

"At ten o'clock in the morning? Course I ain't. Sandwiches'll turn dry and curly. I'll make them in good time, Ronnie, don't you worry. I know what I'm doing." And she went back to her paper.

"Yes, Mum."

There was nothing for me to do and Mum had made it clear she didn't need any help, and as our guest of honour wasn't going to arrive until three, I went away and turned up half an hour before. Mum was in the kitchen, preparing the food. Sandwiches, tomatoes, pickled onions. She'd made a carrot cake, iced it and got out the best china tea-set.

"You've done well, Mum," I said.

"Don't I always do the best for my boys?"

"Course you do, Mum." I bent over and gave her a kiss. "Course you do."

The front door opened and Reg called out, "Mum?"

She wiped her hands on a towel, took off her apron and gave me a big smile. I followed her out the kitchen.

Reg was standing at the middle of the sitting-room, smiling his head off. Judy was next to him, wringing her hands. As soon as she saw Mum, she broke out into a smile and walked towards her, arms outstretched, as if she'd been waiting in the wings and was now going on stage.

"Mrs Kray," she said, "I'm so pleased to meet you. Reg has told me so much about you."

"Miss Garland – "

"Oh, please, Mrs Kray, call me Judy. All my friends call me Judy. You really have to call me Judy." She gave out a schoolgirly giggle and clutched Mum's hands. Then she took off her coat and hung it over the back of an armchair.

Mum said, "Let's sit down, shall we?"

We sat down. Me and Reg on the settee, Judy and Mum in the armchairs.

"Tea, Judy?"

"Oh, yes, please. Tea. Oh! Sandwiches – "

"Ham and mustard."

"I am a lifelong devotee of ham and mustard sandwiches."

"Reg, give Judy a sandwich," Mum said, picking up a small plate and handing it to her.

Reg leaned forward, picked up the plate of sandwiches. "Have a sandwich, Judy."

"Ron, tomatoes."

I offered Judy the dish of tomatoes. Once she'd taken one, we helped ourselves.

Judy nibbled on the sandwich, and played with her tomato, but didn't bite into it. She put the plate down and drank some tea. 'Though, I noticed, she didn't drink. She sipped, put the cup down, sipped again, put the cup down.

"You must be very proud of Reg and Ron, Mrs Kray," she said, her eyes flitting around the room. "They've achieved so much."

Mum gave a little smile. "My sons own London."

"Everywhere I go," Judy said, "your sons' names are on everyone's lips."

"What mother wouldn't be proud of that?"

"Mum – "

"Well, Reg, she's right."

I said, "We couldn't't've done it without you, Mum."

Mum ignored me. "Another sandwich, Judy?"

"Oh, I've not finished this one yet," she said. "I don't eat very much." She reached down to get at her plate of half-eaten sandwich and untouched tomato, fumbled and dropped everything on to the carpet.

"Oh!" she said, jumping up and knocking the cup of tea. So that went the way of everything else. "Oh! Oh! Mrs

Kray! I am so sorry!" Tears ran down her face. "What can I say? Here, let me help you. Oh, I'm such a clumsy fool –"

"It's all right, dear," Mum said, going into the kitchen for a cloth. "Sit yourself down."

I went in to help her. "She's nervous, Mum," I said. "She's not very well."

"Ron," she said, not looking at me, "it's all right. Accidents happen."

But I could tell she wasn't very pleased. After all the trouble she'd gone to with the best china and everything.

We went back into the sitting-room. Judy was now in a flood of tears. Reg had his arm around her, trying to comfort her. Mum got down on her hands and knees to clear up.

"Let me do that, Mum," I said.

"Ron," she said, trying to control her anger and pity, "I said, didn't I, it's all right."

And then Judy stopped crying and opened her mouth. *"Somewhere over the rainbow –"*

Mum's favourite song of all time. Reg must've tipped her off. Mum stopped clearing up.

" – way up high –"

Mum closed her eyes and swayed to the music. She was in another place, another time, a young woman again. Judy leaned over and clasped Mum's hands. Mum opened her eyes and stared at Judy, watching her sing her favourite song.

" – And the dreams that you dare to dream –"

And then Mum joined in. She didn't have a great voice but she more than made up for it with her memories, her love for us two boys and the joy of singing with the greatest film star in the world.

" – Someday I'll wish upon a star –"

Reg and I sat back, watching. We smiled, both of us moved by the scene. Our Mum was duetting with Judy Garland!

When they finished, none of us moved. Everyone

wiped their eyes.

"C'm' on, Mum," Reg said, getting up, "sit here for a minute."

While he helped her into her armchair, I finished clearing up the things.

When I came in from the kitchen, Judy was on her feet. "It's time I went," she was saying. "Mark will be wondering where I've got to." She put on her coat. "Reg, will you be a darling and take me back to my hotel?"

"Course I will, Judy."

"Mrs Kray," Judy said, giving Mum a big hug, "it's been such a wonderful experience to meet the mother of two of my closest friends. Thank you so much for inviting me into your home."

After she and Reg had gone, I was helping Mum do the washing-up. "Well, Mum, what did you think? Did you like her?"

She gave a little sniff. "She's a frightened little thing, too skinny," she said.

When Reg returned to Vallance Road later that evening to see what Mum thought, she said, "I've said all I have to say."

And that was that. Violet never spoke again of the day she met Judy. But when I think of the two greatest women I've known, I think of that afternoon and I shed a little tear.

Nothing

by James Dart

Total and complete emptiness. It was as if Ivy had lost her senses. She tried to scream but no sound came out. She couldn't even feel the muscles of her jaw move. It wasn't that she couldn't move. There was nothing to move. She could not feel her body at all, only the terror bubbling within her, the fear of eternity in this void. She would have cried if she had tears to shed, or eyes to shed them from. Still her mind rattled. The silence seemed to be consuming her.

Ivy's eyes snapped open. The creaking of the boiler and rain pattering on the window told her that she was back in her room. Tears streamed down her face. Her fists were clenched so tightly that they threatened to pull apart the old scars on her wrists.

Usually her bad dreams were about her days in school. The sound of mocking laughter and horrible insults would echo in her mind and she would feel the bruises on her arms again. She would be in a full classroom again. Like always, the seat next to hers was empty.

This was different, though. She wondered if this would be the norm from here on in. After all, she had not been in secondary school for years. Being bullied wasn't really something she was afraid of anymore. Maybe those nightmares were finally tapering off, only to be replaced with nightmares where she lost everything she had gained since then and was totally and utterly alone. Just her luck.

She focused on her breathing, and gradually the tension leaked from her muscles until she felt quite relaxed. At least she was away from there now. She had friends here at Uni.

There was no noise from the other rooms. Ivy sighed with relief. She usually made noises in her sleep when she had nightmares and the walls in the dorms were thin. Her dorm-mates never said anything even if she had woken them up. Ivy smiled to herself. They would never admit what a burden she was. She loved them for that.

* * * * *

Her alarm clock blared at half past six. She was hesitant to go outside and be exposed as the girl who had woken everybody up in the middle of the night because of her bad dreams. Again. But she had a lecture to attend, so she gathered herself, dressed and opened the door. When she was not greeted by the usual sound of her friends' voices and the clacking of plates and cups, she groaned and cupped her face in her hands. She knew it, she had made them oversleep.

She knocked on the next door along in the dorm, Barbara's room. Nothing. She knew how irritating she was being, but she forced herself to knock harder. Barbara did not come out.

Ivy crept along the hall, knocking on each of the doors in turn. Harriot. Jessica. Racheal. Lola. There was no answer from any of them.

She went to the kitchen to get a drink of water.

Where were they? They wouldn't just leave her. Would they?

She poured the water from the tap, turned it off and drank it down in one. She felt a little refreshed.

No, of course they hadn't abandoned her. They must all have gone down to the lecture already, to catch up on studying. Yes, that must have been it. She was being silly again.

Ivy went back to her room, the heavy dread lifting from her shoulders, grabbed her bag and threw her books inside. It was heavy but she usually managed.

On her way out, Ivy saw that she had left the tap

running. Funny, she was sure she had turned it off, very sure. She remembered doing it. She stared at the running water, the hairs on her neck standing on end. Suddenly, she slapped her head and forced herself to chuckle. Of course she had not turned off the tap! Otherwise how could it be running? There was nobody else here!

It would not, after all, be the first time Ivy remembered something clearly and with absolute certainty but which turned out to never have happened. Her mother said that she had an overactive imagination, her teachers called them daydreams. The point was that they were false memories. That was all. Besides, she was still half-asleep. A nice pre-lecture coffee at the student coffee shop would make her feel much better.

Ivy turned off the tap again (for the first time that day), rubbed the sleep from her eyes and went out, locking the door behind her. She clicked her tongue, her mind was playing another trick. As the door closed, she could have sworn she heard water running.

* * * * *

The grey sky seemed to drain any colour from the usually picturesque suburban street on which her dorm sat. Ivy usually got a little pleasure from the sound of the early birds singing their cheerful tunes, but she sighed as she realised that they were silent this morning. In fact, everything seemed unusually silent that morning. There was a chill in the air, one which made her skin come out in goose bumps.

Crossing the road was much quicker than it usually was. There didn't seem to be any traffic at all. In fact, the road was completely empty. Ivy tried to ignore the strange woozy feeling in her gut and joked to herself that she always half-expected people to abandon her. But this was ridiculous.

She saw the first car that day. She sighed in relief. She knew it would have been her imagination. But this car, on the road, was not moving and had no-one inside it. The engine was still running. As she walked down the street, she found another car. And another. And another. All abandoned. All still running.

* * * * *

Even the student coffee shop was empty.

Right down to the core of Ivy's being, she suddenly felt very cold. The beginnings of nausea stewed in her stomach. There were cups of coffee on all the tables. All stone cold. They never left them out overnight. Ivy looked at the bar and saw that the coffee machine was on, all the lights blinking. They were running out of cups like they always did, but there was no-one around.

Ivy clutched at a table to help her stay upright, the room seemed so massive with nobody else in it, she felt like she was in a dolls house. Where was everybody?

She pulled her mobile phone from her pocket and dialled her mum. The phone rang and rang, then she heard her mum's voice. It was the answer phone. Ivy hung up. She called her Dad. Same result.

Ivy's hands enveloped her mouth. Were they dead? Was everyone else on the street, maybe in the world, dead? Was the human race extinct, never to come back? Why was she the sole survivor? What made her different? Was she somehow responsible?

Questions swarmed in Ivy's head like angry hornets, overwhelming her consciousness and mind, stinging her all over with new horrific possibilities and questions. She sat down on a chair, her eyes staring at nothing, her body stiff as a corpse. She felt the chill of a tear rolling down her face as the reassurance and odd hopefulness of fear slowly faded and turned to misery. Her choking breaths became quiet sobs. She curled her knees on to the chair, folding her hands around them, hugging them to her body.

She was alone. She had always been alone. She would always be alone.

* * * * *

Only when the pangs in her stomach became unbearable did Ivy move from that chair. She stood up and walked, barely conscious, over to the counter. She walked around the back and took a croissant, not choosing it, just grabbing whatever was closest. It barely tasted of anything, she had to fight her gag reflex to swallow.

Something touched her arm. She sprang away, dropping the food, looking around. Nothing. But she knew something had touched her. She found herself backing away towards the door. Away from what, she did not know. But something was there. She could feel it getting closer.

Whatever had got everyone else was coming for her.

"No... no, stay away!"

She felt it come closer and closer. Moving ever so slightly slower than she was, savouring the catch. Ivy turned and sprinted through the door, almost tripping as she did. She ran down the deserted streets. Her breath was fast and shallow, a stitch started to form but she did not dare stop. Looking behind her was unthinkable. She did not need to. She could feel the Thing closing in on her.

This Thing had consumed everyone in the street, maybe even everyone in the world. If she hid, it would find her. If she kept running, it would catch her. If she stopped, it would consume *her*. It was hopeless.

Ivy stopped running, fell to her knees, waiting for the darkness to close around her. She felt the Thing caress her shoulder. Nausea clawed its way up from her stomach into her throat as she wondered what was about to happen to her. Her hands shook overpoweringly, her thoughts drifting to eternal blackness, unending nothingness.

Throwing her arms into the air, she screamed. She felt the grip on her shoulder grow tighter but she squirmed and kicked. More invisible hands grasped her, her wrists, her arms, the scruff of her neck. She threw her head back and felt it hit something.

107

Dazed, she realised the Thing would not take no for an answer. It was taking her and that was that.

She pulled herself forward, the tight grip dragging her back. She fell into a sitting position, feeling herself being pulled back toward The Thing.

She couldn't let it take her. She shouted to an empty world. Nothing, not even an echo, replied.

Bracing her legs underneath, she launched herself forward.

The hands lost their grip on her as she piled into the concrete, scraping her arms on the ground. Her head hit the ground with a sharp crack. She rolled down into the road, hearing a grating, mechanical screech.

The Thing was screaming with rage. It wanted her. It would have her.

A jackhammer pounded in her head as she rose to her feet, the world around her phased in and out of reality, humming like a soulless machine. As she stumbled away from the Thing, she risked a look over her shoulder and finally, dreadfully, she saw it.

She saw the Thing.

It was huge. Its inky pulsating darkness spread from the door of the coffee shop right up to the lecture building two doors down and, like an oil slick, across the road into the car park. Out of the front of it, several tendrils writhed and squirmed as they reached for her. The whole thing was reaching for her.

She sprinted away, down the street. She almost fell, her head still spinning from the smack on the concrete. She reached the park and, running through the gates, looked for somewhere to hide.

She came to the bridge over the river. She leapt into the neck-high water, the coldness stabbing all over her body. The place under the bridge was dark. It might not see her. She swam under the bridge, looking up to keep her mouth and nose above the murky water. The cold was burning her skin, her breathing shallow and pained. But she did not dare move.

Her eyelids grew heavy. The wooziness in her head had grown worse. If she lost consciousness, she would drown. Unknowingly, unfeelingly, the mud-saturated water would clog her lungs and suffocate her. She wondered with a bizarre kind of hope if that was the answer. Could the Thing consume her if she was dead?

The bridge made a noise. Something had stepped on to it. For a second, Ivy thought it might come down on top of her. Her head pounded, her brain slamming against the inside of her skull, trying to escape. She wanted to vomit, but held her breath. The noise would certainly bring the Thing right to her. Groggy and slow, she clasped her hands over her mouth, throwing grainy, foul-tasting water into her mouth. The creature did not leave the bridge. It knew she was there.

Ivy felt herself drift. Her eyes closed but she managed to force them open. Keeping her head above the water became harder and harder.

She longed for her bed, her nice warm bed, where she could sleep... sleep... sleep...

There was a splash and a grind of gravel right next to her. As she peered through the tiny slits her eyes had become, she saw the dark shadow of the Thing looming over her. It was going to take her. But she was too tired to care. All of her fear had been replaced with exhaustion and the desire to sleep...

The Thing came closer, reaching out one of its writhing tendrils toward her.

"I don't – "

Ivy lifted her leaden arm toward the Thing, her eyes watering.

"I don't want – "

* * * * *

She woke up in darkness. She felt numb and cold. Although her mouth was dry, the pain in her head was gone, replaced with a droning hum. Where was she?

109

Somewhere dark, that much she knew, and cold. She first thought this was one of her nightmares, but realised that she could still feel her body. After a second of relief, she understood just what an awful thing that was. If this was not one of her nightmares, then it must have been real life.

Was she in the Thing's belly? Was this where everyone else had been? Was she about to be digested? Broken down by whatever the Thing's equivalent of stomach acids were? Or was the Thing just keeping her prisoner? Was she already dead?

She sat up. At least she was able to do that. She noticed that whatever she was lying on was soft and warm – compared to the coldness in the air, anyway. She reached her leg out to one side and found that the softness came to an end. There was nothing beyond but a sheer drop. She did not dare move after that.

She just sat there shaking, crying, contemplating how this was... it. This was it for the rest of her life, maybe even forever.

Would it be easier if she just rolled into the abyss? Get it over with?

She looked around, seeing darkness endlessly in all directions. It was exactly how she imagined it might be. A feeling of numb serenity crept over her. She might even have gone so far as to call it a relief. A relief to be free of all the doubts and horrors of the world, to not have to worry about how people saw her any more, to not feel the everyday pain of living.

Ivy peered over the edge, unsure how far down it was before she would hit the bottom. It could be a small drop – or a massive plunge. Would that do the trick? Or would it take her further into the monster's stomach? She might make things worse for herself.

It would not have been the first time she had done that. In fact, she was always doing that. Saying the wrong thing, doing the wrong thing. Everyone, friends and bullies alike, would look at her like she was a freak. Buried feelings bubbled back up to the top.

Her head ached. The memories of where she had been before were blurry but she remembered most of it. She remembered the awful beast, its hide dark and as cold as the depths of space. She felt so small looking at it. Even the memory conveyed the massiveness of the Thing. Drowning her, dominating her, destroying her.

Maybe if she stood up and jumped head first...

For a while she stared out into the darkness, alone with her breathing. Not even thoughts bothered her as the idea sank in. End it all. One way or another. If she was already dead, then it probably wouldn't make the slightest difference. Anything was better than sitting here all alone, waiting for... something... which might take the pain away or make it worse. She had no idea what the future would hold, whether it would be as bad as now, as bad as being chased by that Thing.

Or it might move her to where everyone else was. Or let her go entirely. The Thing's motives were not clear. Perhaps it was a benevolent, misunderstood creature.

Ivy really had no idea. She was choked with questions, but not a single answer presented itself.

Barely realising what she was doing, she rocked on to her knees and stood to her full height. Her head hit something else. The wooziness came back, her legs were like jelly, she had nothing to catch herself on.

At first, everything was very slow, as if she had jumped into a swimming pool and the water had caught her, gently easing her through. Then her awareness sped up. Suddenly she was hurtling toward the abyss and panic set in.

"No! I've changed my mind! I don't want to die!"

Instinctively, she put her hands out, knowing that it would not save her. The faces of her family, her friends, raced through her mind. She was never going to see them again. This was it. It was over.

Her hands touched something smooth and cool and, before she could think, she was in a mad somersault, winding up on the floor. Many of her questions were answered at once. But she did not understand the answers.

Did any of it happen?

What was the Thing?

How could she have been so stupid?

* * * * *

A key turned. A door opened. A light flicked on.

Beyond the blinding glare, Ivy saw men and women in white coats crowd into the room. They took her by the wrists and held her down.

"It's all right, Ivy, but you need to calm down for us, all right?"

* * * * *

As they could not give her tea or any other hot drink, she settled for water in a plastic cup.

"What happened?" she asked Dr Saeed, a woman with the face of a kind grandmother or a loving aunt. "What was that Thing? Where was everybody?"

"Yesterday," Dr Saeed said, "you were in a major psychotic episode. What did you see? Ivy, what did you see?"

Ivy shut her eyes. The memory was fuzzy. "Like a big, hungry, black Thing. It was awful. Everyone was gone, Doctor." She felt humiliation creeping in. "Was that all in my head? Am I mad?"

"No, of course not!" Dr Saeed held up her hands. "Ivy, relax. There's no cause for alarm." She smiled. "You'll need some medication and once we've cleared you, we'll take you somewhere where you can get the help you need."

Trying to hold back the tears, Ivy turned her head away.

"Your friends were worried about you," Dr Saeed sighed, pointing to the bedside table.

Ivy had not noticed the cards. More than a dozen messages left by friends, all decorated with hand-drawn hearts and smiley faces.

Miss you, Ivy. Get well soon. Jess.

We're here for you, babe. Harriot.

Keeping your place on the couch warm. See you soon. Barb.

"Oh my God! They really wrote these?"

"There are more." Dr Saeed said. "They came earlier but we thought it better to let you rest. They're in my office."

Ivy blushed. "How long was I asleep?"

"A day or so." Dr Saeed smiled. "What happened wasn't your fault, Ivy."

"Will it happen again?"

"We'll put you on some medication and see how you do." She opened her notebook. "Tell me, have you ever had suicidal thoughts?"

Ivy stared at her, wanting to answer but too embarrassed to do so.

"Having those thoughts doesn't make you weak or bad, Ivy. You have to believe that."

"Yes," Ivy muttered. "Yes, I have."

"You shouted that you don't want to die."

Ivy nodded.

"That's good. What were you thinking when you said that?"

"My friends," Ivy said, her eyes welling up. "I never realised they... I want to live."

Flash Fiction 3

Daddy's Girl

by Nick Johns

"Hide, Millie." Daddy's voice sounded in my ear, just like he was here with me, not dead outside the shelter.

One of the Others had followed me into the apartment building.

I thought I'd lost him but when I tripped and fell he heard me.

Boots echo in the stairwell.

I can't outrun him. He is a full-grown adult, a big one, faster than me.

And now he knows I'm here, he'll just keep coming.

The Others always do.

Closer now. Footsteps in the hallway. Just outside the rooms I'd ducked into.

I creep out on to the balcony. The handrail is gone in places and the wind whistles an eerie tune through its missing teeth.

I squeeze behind the rusting air conditioner.

The Other shuffles slowly, cautiously, on to the balcony.

I can smell him.

That's what gives them away, Daddy said, even when they try to be quiet.

He turns, peering over the edge. Yeah, like I'd have hidden there.

I charge him. My shoulder squishes into his back. He teeters briefly on the edge before toppling over.

Turning away, I hear a groan. He's grabbed the railing as he fell and is swinging, one handed, like a leaf deciding whether to fall.

If he falls from thirty floors up, his body won't be a

117

leaf. From this height, he'll be mulch.

What do I do, Daddy?

"Save him, Millie."

But he wants to kill me.

"Remember, Cupcake, there's value in everyone."

I move, but not too near.

"Always pay attention, Sweetheart. Despite their limitations, the Others can be quite dangerous if you're not careful."

Daddy said that when the epidemic started. He was a scientist before the chaos. That's how we survived. Daddy knew how the Others would behave.

I lie down, scraping my belly against the balcony's concrete floor. I lean out over the edge, reach down.

In the Other's eyes I can see, deep within, in whatever passes for his brain, he's figuring a way to kill me, even now.

He hates me.

Why do they hate us? I never understood. Daddy never said.

The Other swings an arm up sharply, tries to grab me.

I swat it aside and grab him around the neck.

His eyes bulge and he scrabbles at my fingers with his free hand.

Finally, desperate, frightened, he lets go of the balcony.

Too late. I have a good grip on him now and, with his falling weight and the twist and claw movement Daddy taught me, I rip his head clean off.

"Good Girl, Millie. You need brain food if you want to grow up to be big and strong."

I must get out of here. More Others will come.

The smell is even stronger now and I'm hungry.

But I must wait until I reach the shelter.

I skip, swinging the head by the hair, splattering fresh blood around the stairwell, like a finger painting.

Daddy was right.

The Others do have value.

Nutritional value.

Find a Quiet Corner

by Nick Johns

There you go love, sugar's on the table. You can't smoke that in 'ere, mind – don't bother me but... Ooh! What you writing? Another JK Rowling, is it? She wrote in a cafe, know that? It's the quiet, see... Of course, I don't like all that wizards and such m'self. OK for kids, I s'pose. My young nephew, now he loves it. Wanted me to get him the books for Christmas – I got him the DVD box set in the end, better for him really, you still get the proper story – with pictures... Still, plenty of money in it – stories, I mean – look at all them famous actors that are in it – the film, that is. That Richard Harris now, fancy him doing a kids' film, after all that drinking with Richard whassname – Burton. Good-looking men, mind you – until the booze got to 'em. But they must have had something going for them. I mean, Elizabeth Taylor married him twice, not Harris, the other one, and she was the most beautiful woman in the world – 'til she took up with that Michael Jackson... Shame, really. Nice boy he was, when he was with his brothers, I mean, not after he started living with that monkey. I ask you, what was that all about? Well, honestly, Clint Eastwood never did that and he had a monkey, didn't he? Different colour, mind you – the monkey, I mean. Although come to think of it, you could say the same about Michael Jackson, eh? Anyway, can't stand here chatting with you all day – got work to do... Write about me in your story, you'll need some real people in it, eh? Well, go on – you'll never make a fortune like that. Write something!

Love and Romance

Golden Siren

by Michael J Richards

In the days when hungry dragons breathed ungodly fire, blond-locked, fair-faced Prince Richard stood on the top of the tallest tower of the castle with his father, the grey-haired, brave-boned king.

"You must take a wife," boomed the king in the howling winds, "to draw my lineage through princely grandsons to many descendants. Then my tired Christian soul can rest with God while my flesh rots beneath your feet. Take Silver, my strong white stallion, leave my kingdom and return when you have a fair and fertile woman fit to be your queen."

And so Richard mounted the king's horse and rode through stormy forests and across sunken moors. He asked of men, whatever their birth, if they knew of a fair and fertile woman fit to be his queen. For while Richard was of royal stock, he knew in his loins that a woman who is strong and obedient, wise and of child-bearing age, who knows that her husband is her master and that her master is her king, is fit to be queen, whatever her parentage, however small her dowry.

But a hard and bleak winter covered the earth and the prince searched without success. Even the majestic sparrow hawk and regal kestrel hid in fear of frost that bit at their talons as they sought the barest food. The crafty fox and conniving stoat lay famished, too faint to eke out even the lowliest of creatures to eat. The friendly hedgehog and white-nosed rabbit clung to each other deep under the wasted grass, so frozen were they that their hurtful prickles and shedding fur were no hindrance to their need for mutual warmth.

And then, one day in the first flush of spring, the season that gives men generous hearts and expectant hope, while resting so Silver might refresh himself, Richard was awakened by the sweetest song in all Christendom. Across the chuckling brook and through the blossom-burgeoning trees, a phantasm of loveliness stood before him, a beauteous vision that he had dared dream of only when he and God were alone.

She was naked, with skin as pale as pearls freshly plucked from willing oysters; breasts as tender as the softest of Mediterranean apricots; lips as red as plump cherries growing in a summer's orchard; and a voice that youthful nightingales, ascending larks and spirited cuckoos bowed to in servitude, knowing that their chorus could never be as fragrant, as loving, as angelic as her single-tuned song.

And her hair! Oh, her hair. It was her hair, her hair, that besotted the alert prince. God, who is praised above all beings, had created goldenness in her hair that alchemists could only dream of in their wildest fantasies. And to say it was silken is to cause the silkworm to lay down his tools and allow his amateur work to decay. And to say it was shining is to force the Sun itself to stand in awed and servile honour.

Richard, despite intending to find a comely and serviceable woman to be his queen, fell in star-gazing love with the golden locks that overflowed to her thighs while she tumbled in the breeze and danced to her improvised melody.

But as he strode towards her to proclaim his undying love and endless loyalty, a black shadow crashed through the oaks and beeches, with flames of fire razing all that went before it. The golden maid screamed. The blond prince cried out. The black shadow roared thunder that, the prince knew, only a dragon can roar. His eyes fell deep into his furrowed brow. His heart was rent. His fear grew sweaty.

Without pausing, he jumped the brook, gathered the

yellow-haired girl up in his arms, waded through rushing waters and lay her down. Then he mounted Silver, urging the mighty steed on, dismounted and left Silver to face the dragon. And while the prince and his sweetheart were running away, the dragon scorched Silver a burnt bronze and gobbled him up, bones, flesh and all.

For weeks, Silver and the dragon an absent memory, the lovers made their way back to the castle where, proudly, Richard presented his new wife to his king and his subjects. "You have done well, my son," said the God-fearing king. "Now I die in peace."

Folk came from far and near to marvel at the handsome pair settling into married life. Richard, which means rich and powerful ruler, toiled and travelled to keep his serfs and villeins hard-working and contented with their lot. Dora, which means gold, stayed in the castle to prepare the homely hearth and marital bed. But, whenever Richard returned to share his bed with his easily won beauty, the hall fire lay unlit, viands and fruit were unprepared and his bed remained cold and uninviting.

For Dora had no wifely arts and no housewifely skills. "Why should I need these things," she trilled, "when I am beautiful and sing like an angel? Isn't that enough for my rich and adoring husband?" So Richard, who once was blinded by Dora's visage and melody, closeted her away and secretly lay with a slatternly woman. And within a year, this ugly drudge, who cooked succulent meals and cleaned dirty pots until they shone, bore him a child.

And when golden-tressed Dora appeared with the baby prince, whose name was Philip, which means friend of horses, at the top of the tallest tower of the castle, King Richard the Blond presented him as his son and heir. But his subjects heard the boy cry like a familiar and saw that his hair was black. So they muttered in undeceived sorrow and rebellious anger, for they had loved Richard's father, the king, and Silver, his strong white stallion. And Richard laughed at their displeasure, pretending he did not hear them. Yet he was afraid.

Voices from the Past

by Deborah Bromley

I was in a meeting when the message came through. An urgent request for help from Social Services. I looked at the property file for the address and found complaints dating from as far back as 1986, reporting concerns about an elderly man living in a remote farm cottage near the village of Honning. The reports were no surprise; I had been involved with many such cases over the years.

I checked the file summary:

1986 – Elderly man living in filthy conditions.
1988 – Windows blocked up with newspapers and boxes. Smell coming from letterbox.
1989 – Complainant worried about neighbour who hoards stuff and sleeps in a chair.
1990 – Eastern Electricity engineer called to property. Lighting circuit blown. Occupier living in filthy conditions.

And the actions that had been taken:

– Notice of Entry served but no access. No further action unless more complaints received. Refer to Social Services.
– Occupier not co-operative. Refused entry. No further action.
– Warning letter sent about court action to enter premises.
– Informal Notice under Public Health Acts to clean and clear property.

Typical actions, but ultimately ineffective. These cases

never get better on their own. Now it was my turn to have a crack and see what I could do. If anything.

I called the social worker who filled in the details from their end. The man was reclusive; he would not engage with their staff. He was adamant he didn't need or want anything from anybody. A psychological report concluded he had "capacity" and could refuse to accept any help. However, the neighbour had been in touch again today and insisted something be done. She said there were clouds of flies buzzing around inside the house and the smell was unbearable. I took the neighbour's phone number and called her.

"I live in the next cottage and it's quite a distance but I can smell him from there. Last time I saw him out in his garden, he was hardly dressed at all and bone thin. I feel so sorry for him. But he should be in a home."

I reassured her that I would do everything in my power to help. Then I went in search of some protective clothing – plastic boots, gloves, waterproof trousers and a boiler suit. It was best to be prepared. I inwardly cursed the colleagues who had left this job unfinished and prolonged the poor man's suffering.

"I've got an urgent case in Honning," I announced to the office. "It's a section 83 – filthy and verminous." A few faces looked up from their work. "Anyone interested?" I knew there would be trainees who'd leap up from their dull paperwork to accompany me.

Charlie smiled and stood up. "Yep, that'd be great," he said and took his jacket off the back of his chair.

"Come on then. I'll fill you in on the way."

* * * * *

We struggled up a rutted track towards Honning. There were fields of corn on either side of the road, tall and ripe. It was right in the middle of nowhere. We soon saw the cluster of former farmworkers' cottages.

One stood out as the likely candidate. A crumbling

127

chimney at the side of the house announced its dilapidation before we'd even had a chance to note the rotting windows, the warped front door and the drooping gutters filled with growing vegetation. The front garden was knee high with nettles apart from a narrow path beaten down by footsteps.

I silently thanked the concerned neighbour.

"Right, Charlie, his name is Arnold Chivens. First off, it's going to smell pretty bad so be prepared. There may be dead rotting things. You won't faint, I hope."

"No, not me."

"Good. This isn't the right profession for you if you've got a weak constitution. I've got some plastic bootees in the back and some coverall trousers and gloves; boiler suits if we need them. Let's just put the boots and gloves on for now."

We kitted ourselves up and approached the front door. I used my car keys to knock loudly on the woodwork. The sound echoed inside.

"Mr Chivens. Please come to the door. I need to check your electricity." I knew from the file he had electrical problems.

We waited.

"Hello, Mr Chivens. Could you open the door for us, please?"

Eventually, I heard a bolt being drawn across and the door creaked open an inch. A rheumy eye appeared in the gap.

"Go away. I don't want anyone coming in."

"We only want to help."

"Don't want yer help. Leave me alone." Then he coughed. And faltered, wheezing and clutching on to the door frame.

"Let me help you," I said, gently pushing the door. It creaked open.

* * * * *

128

I put my arm around his thin frame and tried to support him. He shuffled a few steps and sat down heavily on a lone chair in the crowded hall. His ragged shirt was crusted with food stains. His trousers were threadbare and held up with string. He was struggling to breathe. I peeled off my gloves and bent down to his level, batting away a few buzzing flies.

"Are you all right?"

"I'll be fine," he whispered. "Give me a minute."

His face was grey, his chest heaving, but there was a spark of something in his eyes as he looked at me. I took his hand and gave it a squeeze.

"Do you… Did Anne send you?"

"Who's Anne? Your neighbour? She's worried about you, you know."

"Nah." His eyes sought mine again. "Anne. My daughter. I've been waiting for her. She said she'd come back for me." A tear trickled down his wrinkled cheek.

* * * * *

Charlie and I helped him into his lounge and on to a comfortable chair – he was as light as a feather. Charlie opened the windows to let out the flies, the frames were loose and rotting. I was very worried about Arnold. I knew he was in trouble from the heat I could feel in his hands and the rattling of his chest as he gasped for breath. Two spots of red had appeared on his dull cheeks from the fever.

We sat in the centre of filth. Newspapers were piled high in every part of the room. Cobwebs hung from tattered curtains. The remains of half-eaten meals mouldered on dirty plates. Flies continued to buzz around the room.

We had no mobile phones in those days. I sent Charlie out of the room to look for the phone. An ambulance was called and directions given. Charlie managed to find a cup which he washed and filled with water. I encouraged Mr

Chivens to drink while we waited. I hoped the ambulance would be here soon.

"So, Anne is your daughter? Can I contact her for you?"

"She promised she'd come back." He struggled to articulate the words through his pain.

"It's okay. Just breathe slowly, if you can. Help is coming."

"She went away... "

"Have some more water." I helped him to hold the cup.

"Lost my wife. Only me and Anne... "

"I'm so sorry about that. Don't worry. We'll do our best to find Anne for you."

His panicked eyes and rattling breath forewarned me he was fading. He didn't find the strength to say any more. The ambulance took him to hospital. My last memory of him was his terrified expression as they put the oxygen mask over his face.

* * * * *

He died that night. I knew we had been too late. However, I still had work to do on the case, assisting the Coroner's Sergeant to get a clean-up done and search for documents to find the next of kin. I still had Mr Chivens' words in my head. I needed to find Anne. I wanted to know how she could have left her father like that and done nothing to help.

We hired a firm of specialist cleaners for the dirty work but first I had to help go through all the effects. I took plenty of protective clothing. Bill, the Coroner's Sergeant, was a cheerful chap. We set about our task.

The ground floor was a nightmare of nameless rotting things but we soon realised there were no useful documents hidden under the filth. We cleared the stairs of stacks of newspapers and went to explore the first floor. It was like a different world. A world where a woman's touch was evident. The floorboards were bare but clean.

Belongings were neatly arranged in the rooms but there was no sign of recent occupation.

We discovered boxes of records relating to the family and the house. We began the process of checking. I scanned everything for evidence of Anne.

Bill found a pile of letters. They were tucked at the back of an old desk. Letters to Arnold from his late wife, Elsie. Courting letters from just after the war. The paper was fragile and I had to take care not to damage it. Some letters were addressed to an RAF base in Hertfordshire. Others to a base in Malta. Then a final letter which explained how she was planning their wedding back in England and was waiting for his return.

We found some photo albums. The lives of this happy couple and their friends and family were carefully documented. Each photograph had a date and a note of explanation. But nowhere could I find any photographs of a child. There were pictures of the farm cottage and the garden. Of Arnold holding some giant leeks and a rosette. Christmases, birthdays, holidays. They were growing older in the pictures but still no sign of a daughter.

Then Bill turned up a box with a flowery pattern on it. The inside of the box was lined with pink velvet, silky and soft. Tissue paper was wrapped around each of the photograph albums. I really hoped we would find some answers. Some evidence of their child inside this box.

Bill and I sat on the floor, staring at each picture, checking each document. Anne was born in 1957. A much-loved child for the couple. As she grew into a bonny dark-haired beauty, her parents' joy was evident. Her christening, her first beach holiday, her first day at school, images of her riding a pony. Picnics, swimming galas, school plays. All recorded for posterity. But the photographs stopped at about her ninth birthday in 1966. Blank pages were left unfilled. There were no more happy pictures for us to see.

"Looks like something bad happened." Bill said the obvious.

"She died, I suppose."

"And Arnold doesn't remember, perhaps?"

"But... he was expecting her to come back."

"Yes, but with old age and dementia, your memory gets patchy. Perhaps he simply wiped the daughter's death from his mind. Sometimes happens if it's traumatic, you know," Bill said.

"Yes, I've heard of that. Amnesia. How sad. But he remembered his wife had died. "Oh well," I said, "he probably went downhill after that. Started hoarding. Or just couldn't look after himself properly."

"If the daughter's deceased, we'll have to look for other living relatives. I'll check at the county registrar's office. The wife's and child's deaths will be registered. I'll take some of those photo albums with me, see what I can piece together. Do you want me to let you know what I find?"

"Yes, please, Bill, just for my peace of mind. We've got a long file on this case and I'd like to close it. And I'll need the next of kin so I can inform them about the state of the house. Not much of an inheritance."

"No. But all the family records are important to somebody, even a distant relative. Anyway, let's double check the other rooms in case we've missed something."

We opened cupboards and desks, dressing-tables and wardrobes. There was nothing more about Anne. No firm clues about close relatives. It seemed they were a self-contained family. In their bubble of short-lived happiness.

There was a loft hatch on the landing and we debated whether to bother looking. We found a rickety ladder and ventured up into the gloom. Bill produced a large torch. He beamed the light on to more evidence of this family's loss.

A rocking horse stood in the corner. Next to it was a rack of clothes – pretty dresses and pinafores and school uniforms – arranged in order of size and colour. Toys were displayed on tall shelving. Baby clothes, rattles, blankets and bottles were set out on a low table. I was drawn to a display of her shoes. I realised that every pair of shoes worn by Anne Chivens was arranged on the floor, ending with a polished brown pair of school shoes, barely scuffed. I wanted to cry.

Bill and I agreed to leave it all and lock up. We'd seen enough for one day. I needed time to think about what we had discovered. I descended the ladder feeling deflated. This was the worst part of my job, dealing with my emotions. It was hard to draw a line and keep work problems away from my home life. I shook my head to clear away the memories. But it made no difference.

I lingered on the landing below the open hatch. I could still make out the shape of the clothes rack. In my mind, I pictured the line of little shoes. I realised I felt relieved that Arnold had passed away. Out of pain, at last. Perhaps they were all together now. I wasn't sure I believed in heaven but, in that moment, there was a sense of an ending, threads drawing together in completeness.

Then, without warning, a surge of joy raced through my body. I felt young again, child-like and full of excitement. Next, a cool draught kissed my cheek. It was unmistakeable.

And in my ear the clearest whisper sounded – "Thank you."

A child's happy shout rang through the house, towards the staircase, sweeping into the garden, the cornfields, the pale blue sky.

"Wait for me! I'm coming, Daddy. Tell Mummy I'm coming."

A Ticket to the Moon

by Michael J Richards

Big-hearted Ben, the black-eyed sailor who worships Good-time Lil, goes into The Half Moon Inn to gamble away his salt-eared coins, earned from the week's cruel fishing.

"Inn-keeper," he snarls, slapping two dirty pennies on to the woodwormed bar, "I'll be grateful if you sell me a ticket to the Moon." Clutching his ticket, he passes under the sign *This Way To The Moon* and goes into the smoky back-room.

"Why, here be Big-Hearted Ben," says One-legged Will, captain of the *Floriana*, who once was bitten by a hungry shark.

"It's Big-Hearted Ben, my old bunkmate," shouts Four-fingers Freddie, who once fed an over-anxious piranha with his own liver-spotted hands.

"How goes it, Big-Hearted Ben?" calls High-voiced Harry, who once came too close to an Indonesian pacu fish. "Come settle yourself by me."

"Get out your dosh," chants Charmed Life Larry, who once sang *The Dead Horse Shanty* to a giant anaconda that enveloped his muscle-bulging torso and then unwound itself, spellbound by the musical mariner's recital.

Big-Hearted Ben looks around the dusty floor, the sweating walls and through the dank oil-lamps that light up corners of The Moon, where lonely spiders have crept and cobwebs hung since the days of good Prince Albert.

"Why ain't Good-time Lil here to welcome her old man?" he growls, pulling his wages from his dusty pockets.

"Deal the cards," says Four-fingers Freddie, "let's win

some dosh."

Everyone cheers and calls for more drink. Cards are dealt. Dough is gambled. Charmed Life Larry loses. Four-fingers Freddie claws in his winnings, cackling to a secret tale he tells no man who fears for his life.

Big-hearted Ben swivels his eyes around the shadowy hovel. "I ain't seen Ticket-of-leave Tom for fourteen nights," he said. "Has Old Bill taken him in?"

"Play ya cards, Big-hearted Ben," the inn-keeper says, bringing in jugs of grime-soaked beer, watered ale and turpentine-laced gin. "You be keeping my other customers awaiting."

But Big-hearted Ben stands up and throws his chair aside. "Why ain't she here to make me forget the past sennights, when all I catches is puny pilchard and shrivelled shrimp?" He picks up his coins and leaves his sweat-soaked mates. He climbs half-broken stairs and bashes down the door that leads to the siren who haunts his cabin-rocked dreams. She cries in horror as he appears in the splintered doorway. Ticket-of-leave Tom, as hairily naked as last April when he took a bath, lays upon her, slobbering and writhing.

She pulls at a coverlet to hide her accommodating stock-in-trade. "Oh, Big-hearted Ben," she shouts. "I'm earning my rent. Come back when Ticket-of-leave Tom has had his fill."

"She be an 'ard-working girl, Big-hearted Ben, and a generous woman," says Ticket-of-leave Tom without turning to face the puce-cheeked fisherman. "Many a man 'elps pay 'er rent. You should be proud of Good-time Lil."

But Big-hearted Ben hears nothing but his muscles and bones throbbing like the heartbeats of cannibals he hunted and ate in his piratical youth. "No, Ticket-of-leave Tom," he says. "This ain't the life for you." And he pulls out his silver gun and shoots him twice in the back.

He gazes down on his one true love. "Oh, Lil," he cries, "you are more to me than the price of all the elephants that belong to the richest maharajah. Ain't that enough?" He raises his gun and shoots her in the heart. For, as every Jack Tar from near Levant to far Cathay knows, a pitiless and callous woman is worth only one bullet.

In tear-wracked grief, Big-hearted Ben, the black-eyed sailor who worships Good-time Lil, tears off his shirt to bare his aching breast. With the howl of a trapped whale, he unhooks his boarding-knife, plunges it deep into his weeping heart and falls upon his blood-drenched sacrifices.

Oh Ben, she loved you like no other man she knew. But she had her customers and had to earn her keep so she could wait for your return. And now Good-time Lil waits no more for Big-hearted Ben.

It is written

by Elizabeth Parikh

… she then slithered away enjoying the shifting, warm sand on her belly and forgetting the crisping skin in an instant. A flick of the air advised it would be wise to travel south.

The road from Agra to Doora coated the car's windows, baked its sticky leather seats and filled the engine's throat with dust. The vista stretched, as wide as it was long, unchanging, endless grains of sand slowly shifting through an unspoken hourglass. Iridescent waters appeared and melted. The road burned into the tyres and Lennon, high on LSD, no longer could tell if she was going forwards or backwards.

The snake skin by the roadside, curling into a ball of decay, was snatched at by the wind, thrown upwards and deposited on the oncoming vehicle. It hit with a slight thud but for Lennon, an apocalypse had begun. Throwing the car back and forth and across heat that oiled the flat of the road, maps, empty cups and rock samples flew around the spinning machine. Lennon braked hard until only two wheels were touching the road. The car teetered dangerously – a balanced, upright needle.

Lennon had the power to decide whether to stick or twist and, at that precise moment, one successful sperm finally burrowed into her last decent egg. Lennon decided to stick and the car crashed back down on all fours to the road. Fate then spoke directly with an Irish accent; if Lennon wanted to take hallucinogenic drugs, she would be saved each and every time. Lennon thanked Fate for the message and felt safe.

Hari could remember every single moment of his life.

He remembered being held for the very first time. He was sat in the crook of a left arm, and facing him, in his mother's right arm, was the version of himself he had shared a space with for so long.

They had both taken it in turns to kick their capsule, one after the other, and a lifelong love of patterns began. The kick would sometimes be replied with a slight pressure, a hand, a communication from the other side, which made Hari and his brother squeal with delight.

One day Hari's brother stopped kicking. And at the same time, no matter how hard he kicked, over and over and over, the hand never came. Hari put all of his energy into staying awake and kicking. He saw the hand press into his brother but never to him. So he kicked some more.

Now, on the outside and, staring from his mother's crook at the twin that continued to be still, Hari waved his tiny arm frantically. He could see a head, black hair, facing the other way, watching the unmoving baby. Hari waved his arm for as long as he could, and screamed, but the head never turned to him. Lennon was suspended in time but Hari was ready to explore his new world. Nothing would stand in his way.

All through Hari's life, Lennon looked *just* past her only son. In photos, his mother's arm hung round him but her free hand would be groping thin air, looking for something to hold. She was asymmetric, robbed of her symmetry. The shrines around the house, even the treasured statue of Ganesh with his trunk hanging off, now propped up a picture of the dead son. Wherever Hari sat, his mother looked at the empty seat next to him where his brother should have been sitting. Every movement and gesture was twinned with an acknowledgement to the son who was no longer there. Hari took to sitting on stools in the corners of the room so there was no place for his brother.

In fifteen years of growing, Hari measured less than four feet in height and was unlike the rest of his classmates at Jaingara. He had joined in the first year of educating boys and girls together and, over the years, watched his classmates pair up and break down

The closest he came to a kiss was when a gang of children, younger and older, led by a sly-eyed boy named Madan from a younger year group, grabbed him by his ankles and wrists. They carried him across the veranda and stood him in front of Saanvi, the tallest girl in the school. She was a loner, a strange creature, standing nearly six feet in height. Madan yelled at Hari to kiss his new girlfriend, pushing him towards her. In his bid to get away from the gathering crowd, he quickly kissed Saanvi where his head reached – in her middle, which was quickly retold that Hari had put his tongue inside Saanvi's knickers.

But what happened next was to upstage even the juiciest of rumours. Saanvi, a fan of martial arts movies and hater of Madan, decided her time had come. She balled a fist from her large, strong hands and brought it whistling down on the top of Madan's head. She made no effort, simply let it fall with grace. The weight of her arm and shoulder and neck and ribs contributed to the great thud that planted Madan to the ground, every joint in his body feeling the repercussions of this thump as he fell, face down, to the ground in shock. Saanvi flipped him over with her foot, as she had seen in the movies. Madan opened his eyes.

"He'll live," she stated and calmly walked away.

As the crowd cheered for Saanvi, Hari fell in love. This action, by this girl, was the first thing that had even been done for him and him alone. No shadow of a dead brother to share it with. For the first time, he missed him.

This was the story Lennon had always told Hari, her son, whenever he couldn't sleep. It came to him now as he gently made his way to the front of the hall, a roomful of black ties and cocktail dresses giving him a rapturous applause.

A tear fell from Hari's eye as he gingerly stepped on to the stool that had been tactfully placed at the lectern in that great hall. Once again, he longed for his brother. Faces

139

looked up at him with adoration, waiting for the speech, the words that would rush across headlines the world over, new droplets for the fountain of wisdom that Hari had already bestowed on the world. Hari solidified this memory by dedicating his Nobel Peace Prize to his twin, sparking a rush of rumours and theory.

Later that night, as Hari had predicted, Hari was reunited.

Art-Installation Mind-Games

by Michael J Richards

The first time Eugene Slattery seduced his model, Alicia thought she'd never forgive him. As his wife, she believed he should love only her. After all, she told herself, that was what marriage meant – a monogamous allegiance to each other.

When she confronted him, he dismissed her anxieties with a sweep of the hand. While women equate love and sex as confirmations of a meaningful relationship, he told her, men easily separate love from the sexual act. Women, he explained as if she were an adolescent schoolgirl, see the sexual act as a demonstration of eternal love.

On the other hand, a man having sex with someone doesn't deny love for another. For God's sake, Alicia, he bawled at her, it's only sex!

She didn't understand until she confided in Dorcas, her oldest friend, who told her how she had gone through the same years ago with Eric, her own husband. He's a librarian – how bourgeois can you get – and he's the same. But Eugene, well, Eugene's an artist, isn't he, and for Eugene, things are different. When women condemn men for their infidelities, Dorcas explained none too gently, they fail to understand men, especially Eugene and – sighing bitterly – Eric.

So Alicia reluctantly, and without telling Eugene, belatedly adjusted her view of the world and, once she had done that, it didn't take her too long to see it had its advantages. After all, while she always enjoyed Eugene's oversized body on top of her, whenever he finished, something always prevented complete and mutual satisfaction.

And Eugene, damn him, always had a reason, he always had a bloody reason. Either, he had drunk too much wine, which meant he pushed, sweated and grunted a lot but in the end had nothing to show for it. Or, he was tired out from servicing his latest model, so his gestures of affection for Alicia were temporarily half-hearted. Or, he was preoccupied with a technical problem on his latest *oeuvre,* so, while physically everything was working at optimum levels, his mind wasn't in the bedroom when she was.

It never occurred to Alicia, when wondering which excuse he'd give this time, that her dissatisfaction was as much her doing as his. After all, hadn't her mother told her that sex was something women allowed men to take as they needed and it was not something women were allowed to enjoy? A view, never spoken of, borne from her mother's petrifying fear of snakes.

Moreover, everyone had tried to warn Alicia off Eugene. He's hung like a horse, they said, and he never tires of showing it to anyone who asks. He's never satisfied, they went on to add, enjoying her discomfort. If it's got a pulse, he'll have his way with it.

Like all naïve women, Alicia believed she would be the one to tame him. And, like all naïve people, she discovered she was wrong only when it was too late.

By then, she had grown afraid that she'd never get Eugene to love her as she loved him – which, as time went by, changed into a passive frustration that she would never again find life in the bedroom as she had the first time he seduced her. It was only lately that she realised that for Eugene, the thrill of the chase and capture gave him more satisfaction than the consummation of the hunt.

Then, one grey afternoon when she was feeling more than exceptionally ignored, she suddenly knew she'd get more response from the Construction Man blow-up doll she'd seen while surfing the net. It never occurred to her to ask herself why she was googling for such an item in the first place.

And the next day, when she was on her way to the Post Office, daring herself to order Construction Man (£46.99, ideal for personal satisfaction and parties), she walked into some scaffolding.

The two shirtless hunks working overhead, disproportionately alarmed, made her a cup of tea which Eugene could've used to clean his brushes with. Then they sat her down on a pile of bricks and tried to comfort her by stroking her hands and hugging her too closely. They were very concerned that she might sue them for negligence for injuries caused. They hoped, they explained deliberately, they could offer her some compensation.

As she laughed winsomely, their tongues fell out of their mouths. As she unexpectedly felt desirable, they rubbed their crotches. As they put their arms around each other, she played with their pecs.

They carried her to the top of the scaffolding and, to her fluttering surprise, gave her a full A&E examination and healed her in places she didn't realise were injured. They then suggested she examine their construction work – which she did with an enthusiasm and thoroughness that equally delighted them and shocked her.

And so Eugene and Alicia's married life fell into a self-generating, if irregular, pattern.

Every time Eugene hired a new model for a Life Study (more an excuse to navigate another seduction, as far as Alicia was concerned), she trawled and caught a lover. So, while Eugene continued to follow his needs as he had done from the age of twelve, Alicia felt liberated for the first time since her seventeenth birthday.

Each knew, without discussing it, that one was faithful to the other in every other respect. Indeed, if they'd thought about it – and neither did – following their sexual needs freed them from silent repression, secret masturbation, nursed resentment and over-reliance on an expectation of something the other either couldn't or didn't want to provide.

After a while, they enjoyed their *liaisons*, openly flirted with each other, mocked each other's sexual selections. Berating the other in public became their private joke. When Alicia shouted across a dinner party that Eugene was a walking phallus, he would announce that she was a heifer in drag – and at home, afterwards, they would laugh themselves silly over the disturbed reactions of the other guests.

As they poured more wine, they'd laugh at how they had laughed, all the while not noticing that they were invited out less and less and that fewer people were accepting their invitations. If they had noticed, they would've said more fool them for believing anyone could be so louche to think such behaviour was publicly acceptable – couldn't they see it was all just a joke?

Privately, and alone, each despaired that their joke had gone too far and that, trapped, there was no way back without ritualised public humiliation. In the safe seclusion of their own minds, both were exhausted by their art-installation mind-games. All each wanted, but was too frightened to admit to, was the tranquillity of a shared bed that invited no expectation of performance but held the warmth of a conventional, loving marriage.

Elve, Forgive Me

by Chris Wright

The fire in the centre of our tent gave warmth and filled the air with a familiar smoky scent. The ragged sound of Elve's breathing spoke of the great effort it was taking my love to cling on to life. Her time was near.

She was propped on a bed of reindeer furs close to the fire, with our three sons and five daughters sitting or standing close by. All of us were awaiting the inevitable, although some of them were too young to fully comprehend.

My eldest daughter, Rafi, was doing her best to quiet the cries of our new-born infant. The wails grated on my ears as Rafi tried to hush her. It was impossible to think, to focus on Elve or what I was going to do.

"Get the child some milk!" I said, more harshly than I should. "She needs to be fed."

"Yes, Papa," Rafi replied, drawing away.

She had seen only eleven winters and should not have such responsibility on her shoulders. But I would have to ask much more of her than was fair.

A fever had taken Elve shortly after the birth and she had been delirious or unconscious for the three days since. She had fought but gradually she had weakened and the light within had dimmed as I watched, helpless.

Finally, the struggle was lost: her breathing stilled and her face took on a serene peacefulness. A pressure built inexorably from within me until I could bear it no longer and I wept uncontrollably; the strain of the past days venting in a torrent that, once released, could not be stopped.

I'd lost my love. I'd lost my companion and my

strength. With eight young children already, how could I cope with another? My brother already struggled with his own family and caring for our widowed mother. He couldn't take on another mouth to feed.

A few hours later, I cradled my new daughter in my arms while the others slept. She gurgled and smiled, unaware of the devastation she had caused – innocent to the hardship and suffering that lay ahead. Part of me wanted to hate her for my loss, another to love her as my last link to a happier life. Gently, I laid her down on the furs and settled to my own sleep. But it did not come easily.

Elve lay in the tent, still. We would not put her outside to freeze in the bitter cold. The light from the low fire played across her face. She looked so beautiful and at peace.

"What would you have me do, my love?" I whispered.

I awoke with my mind set. I knew what I must do and I could only hope that Elve would understand.

It was a bright, crisp day. A fresh layer of snow had settled overnight covering the earth and trees anew. With the help of my brother and our sons, we built a pyre of wood and laid Elve gently upon it. The flames were slow to take but soon they burned high, crackling as they released her soul to rise to the heavens. I would watch for the lights in the coming evenings, knowing that Elve would be among those travelling the road to the afterworld.

As the fire burned down to embers, I harnessed the dogs to my sled and placed my infant daughter, swaddled in furs, upon it. I set off, pushing the dogs harder than I normally would. There was just time to reach the town before dark. The miles passed quickly and, as daylight faded, I saw the glow of the dwellings radiating warmly, lamps lit and placed in each window as was the custom.

Stopping at the first house, I carried my daughter to the door, knocked and went in. A fire burnt in an iron stove, making the room warm and inviting.

"Hello," I called, closing the door behind me.

I waited a few moments before a middle-aged man and woman came in. They were soft, unweathered, used to the easier life of the town. The woman's gaze fell upon my daughter, then her eyes looked to me.

"Welcome," the man said. "Please, warm yourself."

I explained my plight, using all my strength to keep my voice steady. I finished with the question I had dreaded asking since I had awoken that morning. "Would you be willing to take my daughter into your family?"

The woman gasped at my words, a wave of pity crossing her face. She glanced at her husband.

"We're too old to take on a child," she said. "But there is a young couple nearby who are childless. Perhaps they might."

The man led me to a house further in the town and introduced me to another couple. They seemed like good people. But how could I possibly know for sure?

The young woman's eyes lit up as she understood what was being offered. Eagerly she took hold of my daughter, cradling her and cooing over her, a tiny bundle of life.

The young man's eyes continued upon me, measuring, no smile yet upon his face.

After some moments, he took me aside. "My wife has suffered many disappointments. If you are to give us the child, then it must be done completely." He watched his wife and the scene of joy beside us. "You cannot allow us to love her then one day return and wrench us apart."

I felt tears well once more, but by force of will held them back. "I understand. I will not return. You have my word."

The young man nodded. "Then you have my thanks. We will care for her as if she were our own."

A few hours later, I sat by my camp fire away from the town, looking up at the green lights of the Aurora dancing across the sky. I would usually have been fearful of attracting the attention of the spirits on their journey to the afterworld. But I knew my wife was there, gazing down

147

upon me as she travelled and my fear was laid to rest.

"Elve, forgive me."

Flash Fiction 4

Folk Wisdom

by Nick Johns

"Tell me. Will she leave me? I have to know."

"The ancient mysteries teach us that all creation is connected; I can divine your future from any object you own. Pass that jug from your breakfast table."

"Sorry! I thought it was empty... "

"Clumsy idiot! Your fate cannot now be foreseen."

"Why?"

"All men know. It is written... There's no point scrying over spilled milk."

Genesis Revelation

by Nick Johns

"Let there be light, and there was light."

Every light that was ever lit created shadows.

Once created, they do not go away.

From the earliest times, our primitive ancestors knew something that we in our arrogance have forgotten. Myth, story, religion were devised by wise men to pass on this primordial message. We came to believe that these tales were allegorical; we lost sight of the literal truth. Mankind needs light to survive.

Throughout the whole of civilisation, we have used light to drive the shadows away. As science progressed, we developed better and better ways of lighting our world and we forgot them, dismissed them.

But the shadows were only driven off, not destroyed. They receded, resentful, like circus tigers before a whip, but, like the tigers, they waited for a moment's inattention. They lurked, just out of sight, waiting, watching, serried ranks of patient malevolence, distorted phantasms, cruel parodies of our symmetry, biding their time.

Once the light died, they returned. When the electricity failed, millions died, overwhelmed by the sentient darkness, a flood tide no longer held back by our artificial defences.

Just beyond sight, the shadows wait for me.

Hungry for my soul.

Here, now, in the flickering, guttering embers of my last fuel, I know the truth.

Darkness is the natural order of things.

"The earth was without form, and void; and darkness was upon the face of the deep."

Humour

Ellie and Tim

by Deborah Bromley

Ellie walked briskly over the busy crossing, dodging a couple of cyclists, just as the traffic lights turned amber and a bus started to edge over the white line. In her purse was the left-luggage receipt for all of Tim's belongings, which were packed neatly, but somewhat stickily, into his Louis Vuitton suitcase. She'd secured it with a bright pink luggage strap. The guy at Waterloo had commented on the strap. And the weight of the case. She hadn't trusted herself to reply. The chaos of thoughts in her head might have tumbled out of her mouth. She took the receipt as calmly as she could manage and turned away.

That was the day after she'd read Tim's brutal email telling her they were finished. The message explained he'd decided to stay in New York for a further year and had done some thinking (not soul searching or agonised reflecting, she noted) and decided the wedding should not go ahead as planned. That was it. Abrupt. Callous, even. He hadn't even changed the standard greeting at the end of his email: "Kind regards Tim Rawlins, Senior Executive Officer".

She had spent the rest of that evening in a flurry of disbelief, checking and rechecking his previous emails. She trawled through his messages to her on Facebook. She unfolded the one short (but sweet) letter he'd written at the beginning of their separation. Every word was scanned for clues. Then she spent the remainder of the evening studying her own replies to make certain she hadn't given him any reason to break up with her. Her emails and messages were all signed off with the simple, loving message that she was counting the days until 14th June.

Their wedding day.

The next morning, dry-eyed and stone-faced, she had opened the wardrobe and surveyed Tim's belongings. Neatly hung shirts. Carefully matched pullovers. Four pairs of chinos; one brown belt and one black one. He kept his shoes in their original boxes. Identical brogues in three colours. Ellie wondered why that hadn't worried her before.

"I'm a stupid, stupid door mat and I'm stopping that right now."

Then she had fetched his suitcase from the cupboard and laid it on the unmade bed. It was the case she'd bought him to use as cabin baggage on their trip to Dubai. On the bedside table were her pinking shears and a tin of black treacle. It was a half-used tin she had in her kitchen cupboard because Tim had professed a liking for ginger cake.

"Idiot!"

On the floor by the bed, laid out on some newspaper, was a small pile of objects. Mementoes of the past three years of her life with Tim. A chunk from the Great Wall of China. A small, but perfectly formed, replica of a gargoyle from York Cathedral. The ammonite from the beach, found during their weekend in Dorset. A carved dolphin made of sea glass from Cancún. The stone from Antigua with the amber shot through it. Lastly, the smooth white pebble picked up from the park where he had proposed to her. She heaped them up and let them drop. Clunk. Thump. Rattle.

One by one she took down hangers from the wardrobe: the shirts, the Brooks Brothers chinos, two cashmere sweaters, the silk-lined dressing gown, and laid them on the bed. Then she cut each piece of his clothing neatly, but ruinously, with the corrugated scissors, before spooning a dollop of treacle in the middle. That was where she placed her mementoes. Every memory soiled and worthless. She parcelled them up and placed them in the suitcase. The treacle was good for gluing everything together. The belts were squeezed in the front pocket. When her work was completed she noticed the finished result looked like a suitcase full of cocoons. Hibernating until the spring. But these cocoons would not transform into pretty butterflies. Finally, she removed the shoes from their boxes, smeared them with treacle and wedged them tightly on top, soles upwards.

"You won't be walking all over me again, bastard."

It took quite an effort to wheel the case across the bedroom carpet. She tipped it over the top step and watched it crash down the stairs to the bottom. The zips held. The pink strap stayed in place. Then she washed her hands, put on her shoes and coat and called a taxi to take her to Waterloo.

Forty-eight hours since she had been brutally jilted, six hours since she had wreaked her revenge, but it didn't yet feel like she had closure. One last act would be required to set her free from him. The wardrobe was empty of his belongings. Now she needed to empty her mind of the hurt and betrayal and fury. She set about composing her final email to Tim. She hadn't trusted herself to respond until that moment. But the knowledge that she had hurt him back gave her confidence. Otherwise she might not have been able to hold back the desire to rave and rant and accuse and blame.

As she typed, she felt a kind of peace stealing over her. She copied out the instructions about collecting his things. She didn't explain why they were in the left luggage office at Waterloo. He'd have to sweat on that piece of information for a while, before he could get somebody to claim it for him. She wrote about how, on reflection, he had done her a favour. She included the words "callous" and "bastard". Several times. And before she could change her mind she pressed *send.*

Fifteen minutes later the phone rang. And rang and rang. Her heart speeded up. She knew it would be Tim. But she shut the bedroom door and let it ring. She did not want to speak to him, not now, not ever.

Eleven-thirty, after four double gin and tonics, is a bad time to lose your nerve and listen to your phone messages. And listen to your ex-fiancé professing disbelief and begging you to call or read his emails back to you.

She didn't have the courage to call. She looked at the emails instead.

Which was when she read Tim's profound apology for accidentally pressing send before he had completed the message to her with his good news. Explaining he'd been in the process of sending her the email message when he'd been called in to meet with the President and be congratulated on his being offered a Vice Presidency. Which would mean a huge, huge pay rise. And would she ever forgive him for the misunderstanding? Because he wanted to change the wedding to September. At Martha's Vineyard where the firm kept a beautiful property. And his mum and dad were already excited about it and he hoped she would be, too. She would make him the happiest man alive if she would forget his mistake and forgive the hurt he had caused her and talk to him about whether she would agree to a wedding in New England in the fall.

Oh shit! thought Ellie as she wondered how hard it would be to get black treacle out of leather shoes.

Cats 22

by Nick Johns

He loomed over me, the kitchen knife incongruously small in his gnarled, wrinkled hand.

"Cake?" He indicated the delicate Battenberg he had placed on the doily-covered side table just inside the room.

"No, thank you, Mr... ?" I stumbled in the face of the foreign name on the complaint.

"Oh, people just call me Larry. Come in." His heavily accented voice, soft but deep, crawled reluctantly out of his mouth.

As he lowered himself all the way down into a shabby, sagging sofa, I perched nervously on the edge of a creaky dining chair. I looked around once more. No obvious signs up here, and more significantly, no smell.

"We have received a report, Larry... " I began. I found the official "we" reassuring, as if silent, phantom hordes of long retired environmental health officers gathered protectively around me as I embarked on my first solo investigation.

"... a report... about your cats." I twitched an inquisitive eyebrow at him and took out my brand new notebook and pen.

"What about them?" he rumbled.

"Let's start with how many cats you have here in the house?"

He steepled fingers and closed his eyes.

"Well... as such. I suppose. I mean, strictly speaking. None." His eyes flickered open briefly meeting my gaze before sliding away to begin an intense scrutiny of his fingernails, which he started to clean with the knife, snatched up from the table.

"Well," he continued, "one was my wife's I suppose, but she's dead."

"Oh, I am sorry. I offer my condolences. How did she go, if I may ask?"

"Choked on a fur ball, years ago. But my wife is dead too. Not from fur balls, though." He chuckled.

"Larry, this is a serious matter, a potential public health hazard, possible animal cruelty. I need to understand exactly what is going on here."

He studied his toes as I continued. "So, just to be clear, you are saying that there aren't... " I looked at the complaint, "... seventeen cats in your basement?"

He pulled at a stray thread on the arm of the sofa and wound it round and round the knife handle until it seemed that the entire seat might unravel.

"Yes, but, I mean, No, well, they are there, sometimes, they come and go. You know how it is with cats. Seventeen, eh? No. But there's not... " he paused, confused, "... surely not." Another, longer pause and then he puffed out his cheeks before continuing. "Not seventeen, well, not usually. No, definitely. Not the last time I looked, anyway." He gave me a beatific gap-toothed smile.

"Surely you look when you feed them?"

"Oh, I don't feed them. I don't need to. I know what I'm talking about. Not like the damned kids."

"Larry... " I tried to interrupt, but he was on a roll now.

"It's the kids I blame, you know. The kids put cats in the boxes. Students nowadays; they never used to do that sort of thing when I started. It's my house after all. But after the kids started... what can I do? My wife, now, she certainly didn't want cats in the basement. The boxes keep arriving and then I have to go down – to sort out the problem, do you see?"

"Not exactly, Larry. Perhaps I should see this basement."

"Surely, officer, there's no need for that?"

"I may have to insist."

162

He looked confused. "Are you sure you want to? There's no telling what we might find. I really don't go down there much. Only if a new one is howling to be let out."

"Let out?"

"Yes..."

"... of the box?"

"Yes." He smiled again.

"That the kids put cats in... ?"

"No."

"But I thought you said," I looked at my notes, "'the kids put cats in the boxes'?"

"No, and yes," he said "No. Not cats – cat. Only one cat in a box, see? But, yes, boxes."

"So, how many have you got?"

"Which? Cats or boxes?"

"Both. Either. I don't know."

"Neither do I. Now you see my problem with the basement."

I took a deep breath and tried a different line of questioning. "Couldn't you just count them? The boxes, I mean, and that would tell you how many cats. After all, 'only one cat in a box,' you said."

"Oh, that wouldn't work." He shook his head gravely.

"Why not?"

"I only let some of them out."

"What? Why?"

"The others are dead."

"Dead! How many of the cats are dead?"

"About half of them." He shrugged.

"So, how many dead cats do you have in the basement?"

"It's like I said about the others, none, I suppose, technically."

I stood up, feeling that, somehow, this conversation had got away from me.

"I definitely need to go into the basement and see these dead cats. Do you understand, Larry?"

"But you can't see the dead cats. It's dangerous – radioactive. I keep it locked."

"Just go and get the key please, Larry."

As he disappeared into the kitchen, I whipped out my mobile phone.

"Hello, Boss? I need urgent fire service assistance down here... a possible radiation hazard... And the police... The cats? I don't know, I can't get a definitive answer out of this Mr Schrödinger."

Daughter's New Bloke

by Elizabeth Parikh

Couple GINNY and GEORGE aged in their early sixties in the kitchen. GEORGE is arranging crockery. GINNY's chopping veg.

GINNY
Not the old cups and saucers. Get the good ones, George! Here! This cupboard.

GEORGE
You mean the set she half smashed when I wouldn't give her thirty-odd pound for her hair, last time?

GINNY
Don't you dare bring that up. She's making an effort. So can we.

GEORGE
And this one. '*David*'. He'll be another down and out.

GINNY
We don't know that.

GEORGE
Oh ay, got a job, has he?

GINNY
His family have got money. And he's got his own
company. Rose said something about takeovers. If it
goes anywhere she'll be well provided.

GEORGE
Then she can get her hair money from them because
my wallet is staying shut.

GEORGE pats his top pocket.

GEORGE
I'll give you money for your hair, though. You could
get it put on the top in a bun, like you used to. Used to
look really nice.

GINNY
Used to?

GEORGE
Well. It's different now. To how you used to look.
Back then.

GINNY
Give over. And get a knife for the cake.

GEORGE inspects the cake with a look of envy.

GEORGE
Waitrose?

GINNY
Don't start.

GEORGE pinches some cream from the cake behind
GINNY'S back.

GINNY
And keep your dirty fingernails off of it! Cost seven
pounds.

GEORGE
Ginny, they saw you coming! And when Lidl's right
across the way and all.

GINNY
It's my money. I'll shop where I like.

GEORGE
I think you'll find it's my pension.

GINNY uses her vegetable knife to make her next
point.

GINNY
Yes. It is *called* a pension. But what it really is, is
widow's compensation. Because all married women my
age, it seems, lose their husband, and gain an
overgrown baby to look after!

Goes back to chopping vegetables.

Now change that filthy jumper and fetch the milk jug.
Been wearing it all month.

SFX: Doorbell.

GINNY
Get that jumper off!

GINNY (carrying cake, knife) and GEORGE walk through to the lounge. GEORGE sits, reads a paper while GINNY puts down items on a table and exits to answer the door. Enter lounge GINNY. With her is daughter ROSE and her boyfriend DAVID both aged in their early thirties.

ROSE
Hi, Dad.

GEORGE
Rose love. Come in, come in.

GEORGE awkwardly kisses ROSE and shakes hands with DAVID. ROSE puts her handbag down.

GEORGE
You must be David.

DAVID
Yes, sir, pleased to meet you. Thank you for inviting me to your lovely home. I must say I like what you've done with the rose bush outside. You must tell me your secret.

GEORGE
Thank you! You hear that love? You can come any time, David. We've got a spare room. And call me George. None of that sir business in here.

DAVID
And did I notice a metal detector in the hallway?

GEORGE
That's right. That's a middle to top-of-the-range model. Are you into detection?

DAVID
No, but I'd love to give a shot. Find a few coins and the like!

GEORGE laughs amiably but firmly.

GEORGE
You'll not find anything on your first go but yeah, I'll show you the ropes, son.

DAVID
Have you ever found anything historic?

GEORGE
Er, close, close.

GINNY
Mainly bent spoons and battered old cans. Do you want to come and take a seat, love?

ROSE
Carrot cake, my favourite!

ROSE cuts a slice of cake not waiting for anyone else. GINNY tries to make a joke out of it but GEORGE is irritated.

GINNY
Hold your horses, Rose. Let the guest have the first slice.

ROSE
I think you'll find I am a guest now.

Awkward silence apart from ROSE stuffing her face.

GEORGE
Cost seven pounds that did.

169

ROSE
It's a bit dry.

GINNY
Sorry love.

ROSE
You've got the good china out as well, I see. Or what's
left of it.

Awkward pause as GEORGE becomes irritated.

GEORGE
She smashed it, David, last time she were here.
Because I wouldn't give her thirty-five pound to spend
on her hair. Just so you know what you're getting
yourself into.

ROSE
Dad!

GINNY
It's in the past. These things happen. I expect this
happens in your family too, eh, David? Are your
parents local?

DAVID
Currently they're in San Francisco, Ginny, but yes,
they've got a home nearby here as well.

ROSE
David's parents own a construction company.

GEORGE
Very nice, very nice. Well, I might have seen them
around. Do they go in the Nag's Head?

DAVID
Is that a pub?

GEORGE
Just a few streets down. They've got a theme every
night. Curry tonight. You tell them to pop in sometime.
Drinks are on me.

DAVID
I'll pass along your invitation, George.

GINNY
You make yourselves at home and we'll get the tea.
Are you stopping for your dinner?

ROSE
We should probably head back.

DAVID
Oh, we can stop for dinner. It smells so good, Ginny!

GINNY
And there's treacle pudding for afters!

ROSE
With packet custard, no doubt.

GINNY
No, dear, I've made it from scratch. With eggs and
sugar. Give me a hand, George.

Exit GEORGE, holding his newspaper, and GINNY
to kitchen.

In the kitchen GINNY gets the tea tray ready and
GEORGE thumbs through his newspaper.

GEORGE
He'll *pass along my invitation*! Did you hear that,
Ginny!

GINNY
He's seems a smashing lad.

GEORGE
For once I agree! I like him. Could do with another
man around here. Someone on my level.

GEORGE stops on an article and looks up startled at
GINNY.

GINNY
What is it?

GEORGE is flapping and whispers fiercely.

GEORGE
Close the door!

GINNY smiles at the couple in the lounge and closes the
kitchen door on them.

GEORGE thrusts the paper at GINNY and whispers
fiercely.

GEORGE
That serial killer! The bloke they're looking for over in
Flitwick, the photo-fit's just been released! It looks just
like him!

GINNY
Like who?

GEORGE
LIKE DAVID!! Look! Around the eyes!

GINNY fishes out some glasses and looks at the picture.

DAVID opens the door of the kitchen and pops his head in.

DAVID
Any way that I can be of assistance?

GEORGE and GINNY jump.

GINNY
No, love, you just relax and we'll be right with you.

GINNY walks over and closes the door with a big smile across her face. Which drops as soon as the door is closed. GINNY inspects the newspaper again.

GINNY
He does look a bit like him.

GEORGE
I know it does! Should we call the police?

GINNY
It looks like him, that's all!

GEORGE
There might be a reward.

GINNY
So you want him to be a serial killer? Besides, it doesn't say anything about a reward!

GEORGE
I'm just saying, there might be one. We'll see. Probably
isn't him.

GINNY
Any part of you not a bit concerned about our safety?
About the safety of our daughter?

GEORGE ponders this thought.

GEORGE
If this is him, we might get a reward. If it's not, Rose is
probably going to marry very well. Either way we're
quids in.

GINNY
It isn't him. It's just a very unfortunate resemblance.

GEORGE
I'll take care of this, ask him a few questions. It'll be a
good chance to get to know him! You just deal with the
tea tray and act like everything's normal.

GEORGE goes into the lounge carrying the newspaper and
GINNY follows carrying the tea tray.

GEORGE
Rose tells me you deal with takeovers, David, is that
right?

DAVID
Um, that's about right.

GEORGE
So would you say you made a *killing* in the city?

DAVID
Well, yes. I have heard that one before. But I am still human.

GEORGE
And after a hard day's work do you like to *murder* a good pint?

ROSE
Okay, Dad. This is a new level of weird even for you.

DAVID
It's all right, Rose. I'm more of a red wine man. Here's my business card in case *you* ever need my team for anything!

Hands GEORGE a card who drops it on the table.

GEORGE
Red wine. The same colour as blood. Interesting. Tell me, David, how tall are you?

DAVID
Five foot nine.

GEORGE
Do you mind if I just check that?

GEORGE produces a tape measure, DAVID is puzzled but obligingly stands up and allows GEORGE to take his height. ROSE is flabbergasted at her dad's new weird behaviour.

GEORGE
That's about right. Can never be too careful.

ROSE
Dad, what are you doing?

GEORGE
The question is, what were you doing on the night of
the twelfth?

DAVID
The twelfth? I was doing my night shift with the
Samaritans. Yeah, I remember. It was a busy night.
Why?

ROSE
Just ignore him, they don't get many guests.

GINNY turns towards the kitchen trying to ignore her
husband, satisfied DAVID is not a serial killer.

GINNY
I'll get the dinner on.

GINNY exits.

GEORGE
We don't get many guests because they knew you'd be
sulking around the place, with a face on like you'd
chewed a wasp.

ROSE
Well, listening to you and Mum arguing day and night
and then putting on a good show for other people, yes,
it did piss me off!

GEORGE
And your mum and I were pretty pissed off, to use your
words, at you never bothering to pay us any rent. Did
you think it was normal for a grown woman to STILL
be living at home?

ROSE
You think I *wanted* to live here?!

GEORGE
Yes I think you did, three square meals and a bed rent-free. Course you did!

ROSE
Come on, David, we're going.

GEORGE
He can stay! You go! Seeing as we're so awful to be around. Don't let me stop you!

DAVID awkwardly half stands up not knowing what to do.

ROSE
Come on, David.

ROSE snatches her handbag. She accidentally tips up the whole tray and the knife lands in GEORGE's thigh. He cries out.

GEORGE
My thigh! The knife, it's gone right in!

ENTER GINNY to see what the crash was. She sees the knife and DAVID standing over GEORGE. DAVID is the serial killer!

GINNY
You brute!

DAVID is about to pull out the knife. GINNY pushes him away grabs the knife out of GEORGE'S thigh and holds it at DAVID's neck. GEORGE is in extreme pain. ROSE is stunned at her parents' reaction.

GINNY
Don't. You. Dare. Try to hurt my George or I'll chop you up and boil you in my saucepan!! Do you hear me.

DAVID
I didn't do anything! Honestly!

GEORGE
It's all right, Ginny. He's not the serial killer. It was just an accident.

ROSE
Serial killer?

GEORGE
It looks a bit like him, doesn't it?

DAVID and ROSE look at the newspaper GEORGE is holding up.

GEORGE
Around the eyes.

DAVID
I am not *that* kind of… I'm not a serial killer! I love your daughter. I volunteer for the Samaritans!

ROSE and DAVID gaze romantically and hold each other tightly. GEORGE and GINNY look at the mess of the situation.

GINNY
I think we might call it a night.

ROSE, DAVID awkwardly say bye. GEORGE smiles
through pain.

SFX: The front door bangs shut.
GEORGE and GINNY sit in a deflated silence.

> GINNY
> What do you think he meant I'm not *that* kind of serial
> killer?

They both pick up and read DAVID'S business card.
GINNY sighs in relief.

> GINNY
> Oh, thank goodness! Termites. He's just a contract
> killer.

> GEORGE
> Murder She Roach. Clever.

THE END

Let the Games Begin

by Nick Johns

Yesterday the country was thrown into turmoil by the results of the 2117 Party Games.

For almost a century, following the tragic loss of public interest in the years following the 2017 General Election, this great nation has chosen its leaders in accordance with its greatest obsession, public entertainment. Many trace this move to the then Prime Minister's appearance on *The One Show*, where a majority of the population decided that, given the choice, they would prefer to vote for the hosts than any of the contemporary party leaders.

This led to the emergence of the Party Games method of choosing governments that has survived to this day. That method has now, in turn, been challenged following the goings-on in yesterday's contest.

It began in familiar enough fashion. Each team had chosen their champion, genetically imbued with the traditional attributes of old leaders in accordance with the ancient ordinances. The champions had been prepared to contest a series of battle rounds; games drawn at random from the entertainment archives of the golden age of TV and Radio, with one champion eliminated in each round until a clear victor emerged.

In the first game of the contest, *Just a Minute*, the lot fell to Paul Purple. Despite everyone confusingly referring to him as Nigel, Paul began strongly, utterly confident about being able to chunter endlessly, if perhaps senselessly. However, after a Blue Team challenge that the main purpose of the Purple programme had already been achieved and that they had heard it all before, Lord High Adjudicator Nicholas Parsons disqualified him − for repetition. Paul (or Nigel), the Purple Team's champion, was the first contestant to be eliminated.

The second round was *Mastermind*. All appeared to be going smoothly until it came to the Green Team's turn in the black chair. Their controversial decision to have two champions backfired spectacularly. Caroline and Jonathan decided to change places between questions, and also answered on different specialist subjects.

This would have put them at enough of a disadvantage against the clock but, when the second question came in two parts, they changed places early, resulting in the classic *Two Ronnies* problem where each answered the previous question. As a result, they ended the round with fewer points than a post-Brexit UK song at Eurovision. Their challenge to the score led to a testy exchange, punctuated by numerous interruptions, with the Grand Inquisitor John Humphries eventually eliminating both champions of the Green team.

Three now remained. The third round was *University Challenge*. From the start, Tim Yellow was at a severe disadvantage as no-one in the student body trusted his team for historical reasons. When Tim started began asking other teams what he should say and changing his previous answers to align with theirs, he was doomed.

In the final round on semantics, Tim was finally dispatched when, in a withering put down, Quizmeister Jeremy Paxman observed that Tim's Yellows obviously did not know the difference between principals and principles.

The two remaining champions emerged blinking into the studio lights of the final round. *I'm Sorry I Haven't a Clue*, a game for which both appeared ideally suited. With only Theresa Blue and Jeremy Red remaining, the audience settled in for the deciding game.

The initial rounds were scoreless as both contestants appeared equally bewildered by all of the questions posed. Theresa fell back on her mantra of repeating "Strong and stable leadership" in answer to everything, and Jeremy did no better, constantly mumbling in his beard about "The good old days of Stalin and the Gulag".

Finally, in desperation, most of the audience having drifted off to death, the game went to a tie-break, winner-takes-all, round of Mornington Crescent. When Jeremy proved entirely unable to identify any station except Highbury and Islington, and ran off to live in the Socialist Paradise of Venezuela, the game, and the whole of the Party Games, appeared there for Theresa's taking. History beckoned, offering her Blue team another five years in charge (unless she changed her mind early again).

However, instead of travelling to Mornington Crescent and winning, she opted instead to wait on the platform at Euston for HS2 to take her to Manchester. Due to the ever-rising costs of the still uncompleted project, Theresa was declared bankrupt and disqualified from holding office, thus becoming the only champion to lose both the Party Games and Monopoly at the same time.

The Last Will and Testament of Charity Perpetua Love

by Allan Shipham

If you are hearing this, then I have passed on and you have been summoned by my long-time confidant and closest friend, Mr Charles Screwem, to his offices at Screwem, Goode and Harte Solicitors.

I wanted you all to be together so you could reflect on and share the fruits of my wonderful life as an everlasting memory of me. I've had a marvellous time and I want to thank you and let you know that I loved each and every one of you.

Being of sound mind and body, revoking all previous wills, and witnessed in front of Charles's trusted employees, I wish to confirm the following:

1) In line with my wishes and authority, all life insurances have already been collected and all property disposed.

2) My earthly body and those of my beloved departed cats (previously stored in the deep freeze in the utility room) have already been cremated. Our ashes have been scattered in line with my wishes – on the picnic area by the river. I always liked to walk there and it seemed a good location for our final resting place.

3) All accounts have been settled. I don't want a wake, flowers or a monument, so there are no funds remaining for any permanent memorials. Please respect my wishes in this matter.

4) My surviving cats, Oscar and Tumbledown, have been given a care provision.

To my beloved sister Beatrix, life has been kind to us. I gift you the memory that Mum and Dad did their best for us being the only girls, even if you were always the favourite. In time, you will realise the value of this memory. You always did better than me and you certainly don't need any money after Fred died. Sadly, you never visited me in later life when I was ill or when I was in recovery.

I must take this opportunity to confess that it was me who took the diamond-encrusted gold bracelet you thought you lost in a burglary in 2010. I borrowed it. After you called the police and made a fuss, I had to dispose of it quickly and the cash paid for my cruise in the Mediterranean. Thank You.

To my surviving brother Raymond, you were a rock to the family. I will miss you the most. However, your sad devotion to that awful religion and the cronies who worship there is the reason I cannot bequeath you any money. You'll just donate it to fix the roof or buy new hymn books. By the way, it was me who took your hat and coat from the pub in January. It was to teach you a lesson about caring too much for others, while neglecting yourself.

I do regret that you caught double pneumonia walking home in the snow and nearly died. Luckily, by March you were up and about again, healthier than ever. Ray, please look after yourself.

To my best friend Janice from the Darby and Joan Club. I thought about it long and hard and the best gift I can give you is deliverance from deception. We had the greatest time together and I always enjoyed your company and dancing.

Much funnier, I also enjoyed Timothy's company and it would be wrong of me not to tell you about our romantic liaisons before you both get married next year. Of course it takes two to tango, but in some ways you don't help yourself. I hope we can still be friends in the next life.

To my bridge club friends Edwina and Martha, I gift you a guilty secret. You'll notice Charles didn't invite Angelina today. Angelina and I worked out several cheats when we first started playing cards. If either of us tapped our ear we went strong on Diamonds, and so on.

Sorry. We fleeced more than two thousand pounds from both of you over the years. As you both know, I was a heavy smoker and drinker, so I'd like to thank you for helping to fund my habits. I hope you're not angry with either of us. Angelina knows about my intention to confess, so it's likely you'll not be able to get hold of her for a while.

And now to the distribution of my estate. I've decided to gift one thousand pounds to each of my eleven nieces and nephews and their partners. Sadly, I never bore any children but I enjoyed seeing you all grow up and live your lives. It isn't much, but a small amount can make a big difference in some people's lives.

In my memory I'd like you to gift it all to local charities so you can see the rewards of helping others. It may seem like a kick in the teeth, but as my name is Charity, I hoped you would remember your sad old aunt with this act of kindness.

Finally, a special clause which allows for the following provision:

If any of my surviving family or friends contacted Mr Screwem about providing a home for my cats, they were to receive five hundred thousand pounds and custody of Oscar and Tumbledown. There were strict conditions about their care, but the cash always came with the cats. If you are hearing this paragraph, it means that my beloved cats were forgotten about in your daily misgivings.

I wish I could see your faces. How awful to come to the reading of a will in the hope you will be bequeathed, only to find I actually took something from all of you, even if it was only your dignity.

The whole residue of my considerable estate is therefore bequeathed to a local cat sanctuary, a worthy, cash-strapped organisation that provides a safe haven for unwanted cats. The plan is to refurbish and rename the sanctuary, using my donation. It is to be called the William Shakespeare Cat Sanctuary. Oscar and Tumbledown will be looked after by the caring staff until they join me and the other cats.

It's not widely known, but William Shakespeare hated cats. I hated his work, so I thought it would be incongruous and slightly amusing to name a cat's home after him.

In witness this Twelfth Day of October 2016.
Signed by the said as *Charity Perpetua Love*

Flash Fiction 5

Mr Tick-Tock Man

by Nick Johns

"Tick-tock," he whispered.

And I knew.

The tales of the maker were true.

It was time. He'd come for me.

Huge liver-spotted hands, thinly covered with greying parchment skin, long sharp nails with an unnatural sheen, approached slowly, precisely, like a diamond-cut escapement.

"Tick-tock."

He moved closer with a waft of slick, sharp machine oil. His single, glittering lens studied me.

As I counted my final imperfect minute, seconds stretched like taffy, I knew I'd never mark another faulty hour.

He thrust his sharp, shining instrument deep inside me, twisted once, withdrew, then smiled.

"There. All fixed, little clock. Tick-tock."

Murder in the Night

by Nick Johns

My first killing blow had missed.

I cursed my nocturnally dulled reflexes. The element of surprise was lost. My victim, forewarned and alert, was concealed in the shadows.

He could hide in inaccessible places, hoping to outlast me. This was not my first kill, I knew how this deadly game was played. I must act silently. Noise would rouse new enemies.

I froze, listening intently. Blood hissed in my ears. I crept, in stop-frame motion, to flush him out. He suddenly flew at me. I raised my newspaper for the messy dénouement.

WHAM!

Eventually the insomniac always beats the fly.

Poetry

All Love in a Day

by Pat Aitcheson

At dawn we played at love with sly smiles and heated
glances butterfly touches on my arms a thousand
possibilities.

In the morning we laid in love wrapped in hot kisses and
whispered words a thousand silent candles our only
witness as we rode the waves.

As the sun reached its zenith we declared our love our
future before us with fair wind and full sail.

In early afternoon we multiplied our love but watched it
scatter to the winds the storm that almost broke us.

In later afternoon we gathered up our love patched made
new and set sail again wiser.

In the twilight our love became safe harbour when our
strength was almost gone.

In the evening we prepared our love to go where we must
follow when sunset comes.

Now only I remain in lonely night.

Clear warnings

by Allan Shipham

What was that noise that woke me from my sleep
From a faraway land after counting those sheep?
It sounds like a burglar tearing through my garage,
Upturning boxes and buckets, a phantom mirage.

It's happened before. I looked out of the window,
clutching teddy and blanket, I saw a strange weirdo.
His cheeks were rosy – but he wasn't Santa Claus –
He flapped like a pandemonium of macaws.

His clothes stand out brightly against the dark silver light;
strange that he only visits in the middle of the night.
His beady eyes striking, standing out by a mile,
there's no sign of comfort, no sign of a smile.

His face is a sad face, broken and smudged,
he waits your attention, he wants to be judged.
His hair is green like the peas in a pod,
you're frozen with fear, he commands like a god.

Step away from the window, step away from his gaze,
let's hope he didn't see you in the glimmering haze.
You want him to go and find another to scare,
but you know you'll feel bad, another child cursed to stare.

Some say he's a drunkard destroyed by love,
That he killed someone (all they found was a glove).
The smell of stale face paint follows wherever he goes.
Meet him and you'll get chills from your head to your
toes.

194

He's been seen with a chainsaw, been seen with a knife.
Take care to avoid him for fear of your life.
Are you sure that that creak from under your bed
was only the floorboard, not something to chop off your
head?

And now I'm grown up with a moustache and beard,
I don't see him often, thank God, 'cos he's weird.
I wonder what he's doing. Where he can be?
A creak of a floorboard – something cold touched my
knee!

I expect that you're wondering what scares me the most,
while you're drinking your tea and eating your toast.
My warning is clear. Take care when in town.
You'll probably meet him, the notorious, urban, flesh-
eating clown!

Between the Lines

by Jayne Osborn

Dear Mum,

Thanks for the parcel, the socks fit a treat.

(*I wish you could send me some good things to eat.*)

It isn't too bad here, things could be much worse.

(*This is the worst place in the whole universe.*)

Guess what, Mum, the lad next to me in this trench –

(*We don't get too close here, because of the stench.*)

– his mother has got the same birthday as you.

(*Oh, Mum, I'm so scared – I don't know what to do.*)

It's great, getting up every day at sunrise.

(*I hate to deceive you, this stuff is all lies.*)

You always say, "Things aren't as bad as they seem."

(*The shelling goes on till I just want to scream.*)

We all hope to come home, the sooner the better!

(*We live by the hour, this may be my last letter.*)

There's a football match soon; they're calling a truce.

(*The enemy's our friend for a day. What's the use?*)

I hope everyone's well, Mum, I really must go –

(*This is living Hell, Mum, you don't want to know!*)

I'm dying to go to...

(*I'm going to die, too...*)

Glossing over the Facts

by Jayne Osborn

Remember True Confessions on the radio,
when people told of dreadful things they'd done?
Owning up to misdeeds isn't easy, though.
For those who sit in judgement it's more fun.

The worst I heard was called "The Goat Confession",
where two men hurled some wood right down a shaft.
They'd been on quite a heavy drinking session,
and thought this prank was great. They stood and laughed,

but not for long. The wood, a railway sleeper,
was fastened to a length of sturdy chain,
to which a goat was tied. The shaft was deeper
than they had thought. The goat? . . .Not seen again!

Now I'm going to tell you my confession.
You'll think I didn't show much common sense,
but I was young when I made this transgression,
and that's all I can say in my defence.

The general store in – "BLANK" – was really quiet
on the day this awful incident took place.
It's just as well, there might have been a riot.
I'm not saying where it happened, just in case.

I had a flat that needed to be painted,
so went to buy the stuff, but thought the smell
might permeate the food and leave it tainted,
which was stupid; tins of paint are sealed up well.

Nonetheless I put some white gloss in my trolley,
in the place a little toddler's meant to sit,
but all too soon I'd realise my folly –
at the time it seemed to be a perfect fit.

But as I walked along, the can vibrated.
It was lined up with a leg-hole when I stopped,
and what I said means "Oh dear!" when translated,
as the can slid through the gap and duly dropped.

The next few minutes happened in slow motion,
or so it seemed. The lid came off (of course!)
and abject horror was my one emotion
as the paint shot all around with mighty force.

But close by, in this aisle, was just one person,
a woman who was clearly unaware
of what had happened. Things were soon to worsen,
for I noticed blobs of paint stuck in her hair.

She hasn't noticed yet – I can't believe it!
There's white gloss spattered all across one shoe.
The tin is on its side; I can't retrieve it,
the paint's still running out. What shall I do?

Things were looking blacker[1] by the second:
She had a suede coat on. Oh, please God, no!
I thought about it then I quickly reckoned
that my wisest course of action was to go.

She'd moved her trolley on, still busy shopping,
and the wheels had left a crazy painted track.
I dashed toward the door, just briefly stopping
to stare at all the splodges on her back.

---

[1] Actually a lot of things were looking whiter!

I've often thought of that poor woman, finding
her coat was ruined, shoes and hairdo too.
I'm older now, and hardly need reminding
that fleeing was a dreadful thing to do.

But I was scared; I hadn't got the money
to make amends for all that paint I spilt.
Hearing true confessions might seem funny,
but the perpetrators have to bear the guilt.

In the meantime I've just put it all behind me,
although it's caused me nightmares, to be frank.
But I'll pay up if my victim ever finds me,
. . . and identifies the mystery town of "BLANK".

Lessons Learned the Hard Way

by Jayne Osborn

Some things in life aren't what they seem,
as Thomas Gray's *Selima*[2] found:
the cat who saw a golden gleam
it coveted; she sadly drowned.
Gray's warning: "*Be with caution bold.*
Not all that tempts your wand'ring eyes
and heedless hearts, is lawful prize;
Nor all that glisters, gold."

Such sound advice, yet often spurned
by those whose driving force is greed,
for many men have never learned
the variance of "want" and "need".
In 1896 they fought
and cheated, lied, for wealth untold.
The Klondike yielded what they sought:
that lustrous precious metal – *GOLD* !

But many things aren't what they seem,
including minerals and ore,
and some men found, inside the stream,
just worthless sulphide, nothing more.
They didn't know that it was fake;
it looked like gold – and how it gleamed!
Those men were fools. Their big mistake
was thinking things were what they seemed.

---

[2] *Ode on the Death of a Favourite Cat, Who Died in a Tub of Goldfishes*, Thomas Gray (1716-1771)

Mother Care

by Jayne Osborn

"I'd like a pair of those rubber gloves,"
says my Mother (aged eighty-four),
and during the next ten minutes or so
says the same thing four times more.
The "rubber gloves" are just napkins, which
are folded and stacked in a pile;
the waitress brings us a pot of tea,
with a false and indulgent smile.

This is the mother who taught me well,
to love literature and art,
who can't remember my children's names
but knows "Adlestrop" by heart.
"She used to be so intelligent,"
I'm often heard to explain.
"Until a couple of months ago
there was nothing wrong with her brain."

In her day she'd been a magistrate:
highly respected, and clever.
Retirement had brought new challenges;
she was always busy. However,
we leave the café, our roles reversed;
me, with a child whom I love.
I denounce senility and then...
wipe my eyes on a rubber glove.

Putting My Affairs In Order

by Jayne Osborn

A friend has told me I should do this, just in case I die.
I've thought about it quite a lot, but still can't reason why.
Well, never mind, although it's hard, here goes; I'll have a
try.

* * * * *

I've cast my mind back years: my first affair was with Joe
Green.
He liked to make love in the open but I wasn't keen.
Alfresco sex is not for me; what happens if you're *seen*?

The next one was a chap called Stan; now Stan was four
foot ten.
Although he was quite nice I really *do* like taller men,
and after several dates I thought, 'I won't see him again.'

I think that number three was . . . wait a minute . . . it was
Bob.
He knew which buttons he should press, but wouldn't get a
job,
and so he had to go. The man was just a total slob.

Hang on, I may have got it wrong, and Bob was number
four.
Or was it Henry, Claude or Miles? I really can't be sure.
This "putting them in order" business really is a chore.

My eighth affair – or am I up to seven? – that was Jim,
a famous politician, so I've used a pseudonym.

He told me lies (yes, really!) so I very soon dumped him.

Now where exactly does Fernando feature on this list –
the one I met that Christmas. (Think I passed out when we kissed.
I only went with him the once and that's when I was . . .
drunk!)

Before – or was it after? – him, came Ivor, on that cruise.
I don't remember much except we sank . . . a lot of booze.
He'd moan and sweat excessively when . . . taking off his shoes!

I *could* count backwards, starting with the latest, I suppose.
The trouble is, there are a few of which nobody knows.
I'm still not sure this is the kind of stuff I should disclose.

I don't see why I need to sort this out before I die.
When one's "affairs are all in order" who d'you notify?
Who'd want to have a look at my dramatis personae?

It's quite ridiculous. I think my friend has been misled.
There's only one thing people want to know, when you are dead,
and that's how much you've left them. I'll update my will instead!

Severance

by Jayne Osborn

I stoop to catch a lemon rolling slowly down the street
and marvel at it. Recently, this fruit was on a tree
and now it's lying in my hand, so perfect, and it's free!
(Like me – except for "perfect" – but this feeling's
bittersweet.)

I've fallen from my family tree, the place in which I grew,
to be the person I am now, as circumstances change,
but no-one plucked me, nor the lemon; somehow we both
knew
instinctively the time was right to drop, and go. It's
strange.

Ulterior Motive

by Jayne Osborn

Oh, you *must* come and visit me, Darling,
in this charming old cottage of mine.
      I have a nice guest room,
in fact it's the best room,
– the view from it's simply divine!

There's tranquillity here in the country.
You will love it; the air is *so* clean.
      We'll stroll at our leisure,
      deriving much pleasure
from being surrounded by green.

Lots of wildlife abounds in the country,
and meandering rivers as well.
      It's all butterflies… bees…
      hedgerows… birds… fields… and trees.
Please come – *it's as lonely as hell!*

Flash Fiction 6

Night of the Hunter

by Nick Johns

"All alone?"

Three shapes solidify from the gloom.

My heart beats an eardrum tarantella.

White, laceless Nike Airs. Adidas hoods not hiding avaricious, feral eyes.

A knife glistens orange in the sodium light.

"Best we carry your money, eh lads? Safer." The sneer has yellow teeth. "After all, the night's a dangerous place."

My fingers urgently caress the feathered totem.

Overhead, pinions beat, inky shadow staining the glistening asphalt.

A looming figure settles behind them.

Unblinking obsidian eyes regard me.

"Hunt!" I command.

The first talon flashes.

They flee.

I wait, listening, until peaceful night smothers the third truncated scream.

The Old Methods

by Nick Johns

"This is why I hate taking a break. When I get back, there are always problems. Our business is a mess. Look at the figures. Takings are down. Volume is down. Turnover is down. What the hell have you three been doing while I was away?"

He addressed each of his brothers in turn.

"You were the first of us to go global, but your sector of the firm has almost disappeared. Viral marketing? What does that contribute to our bottom line?

"And what about you? Still spending all your time messing about in the Middle East. You should know that it doesn't generate the amount of business that it used to.

"And finally you. OK, Africa has been steady, but no results anywhere else, just projections for India, Bangladesh and the rest of South East Asia; and what are you doing to exploit the potential of China?"

His angry gaze swept the room.

"Enough! We're going back to the methods that made this partnership feared throughout the world. You're going to get back out into the field and raise your numbers. It starts today. Come on, let's go!"

He swept out, the three of them hurrying in his wake.

"This business is going to hell, and if it's the last thing I do, I'm going to make sure it gets there," he screamed, mounting his pale horse.

Contributors

Gordon Adams, a marketing consultant living in Buckinghamshire, is the author of two non-fiction books on career change, both originally published by Infinite Ideas: *Overcoming Redundancy* (first published 2009) and *The Great Mid-Life Career Switch* (2010). The second edition of *Overcoming Redundancy* was published in 2015 by New Generation Publishing. Northants Writers' Ink's second anthology *While Glancing out of a Window* contains four stories by Gordon and were his first published works of fiction. Another two short stories have been included from Gordon in this anthology.

Pat Aitcheson has been an active member of Northants Writers' Ink since 2015 and joined the Ninja Writers online group in 2016. Her science fiction novel *Looking for Heaven* was long-listed for the Bath Novel Award 2016. Her short story *All the sands that touch the sea* won first prize in the H E Bates Short Story Competition 2016. In 2017, her short stories have been published in a local monthly lifestyle magazine *Barton Today*. Currently she writes fiction, poetry and non-fiction for a number of publications on the writing site Medium, as well as her weekly blog at 2squarewriting.com. While science fiction and fantasy are perennial favourites, she reads and writes in a number of genres. She lives in Northamptonshire with her family. A keen gardener, she often uses plants and flowers as images and symbols in her work. She writes to take the reader into different worlds seen through another's eyes, using the magic of words.

Deborah Bromley is a hypnotherapist specialising in Life-Between-Lives (LBL) hypno-therapy, a deep trance process that connects you with memories of your life as a soul, in between incarnations. She trained with Dr Michael Newton, bestselling author of Journey of Souls and Destiny of Souls. Deborah contributed to Dr Newton's subsequent book, Memories of the Afterlife. She is the author of two novels, The Channelling Group and The Walk-In. Both are self-published and available from Amazon and other online booksellers. She is currently working on the final part of this trilogy. Deborah wants to reach out to a wide audience who love paranormal fiction and share an interest in alternative realities. She has a passion for reading and is never without a stack of books on her bedside table – most likely to be either crime thrillers or romantic fiction. She has discovered the pleasure of writing short stories from her membership of Northants Writers' Ink and hopes to assemble enough material for a collection in the future.

James Dart writes: As long as I can remember, I have had a passion for storytelling. As a child, I was often lost in my imaginary worlds, and shared them with my friends. So when I grew up, writing seem like the obvious thing to do. I have great interest in studying law as well and have a degree in the subject from the University of Buckingham, as well as an LPC and LLM, both obtained from the University of Law. In between these two periods, something happened which would change my outlook on life. In the same week, my mother developed cancer and my father was told by a doctor that there was 'something' in his lungs. While both were ultimately fine, I shall never forget how I felt during that week. I had an existential crisis. I realised the unfairness and the fragility of life. But, after a while, I decided that this fragility was what made every moment precious. It was these sudden realisations that were the primary inspiration behind my story in this anthology. I hope you enjoy my story and you'll let me tell you another some day.

Beth Heywood was born in Lancashire many moons ago. She has travelled throughout Europe, America and the South Pacific, where she spent 35 happy years. She is now happily settled with her husband in Wellingborough. When she is not writing, reading or gardening, Beth enjoys walking around Northamptonshire, exploring its many secrets. With her husband's help, Beth hopes to have her website up and running very soon. Do drop by at her place at www.bethheywood.com.

Nick Johns is a Welshman, living in exile in Northamptonshire. As a boy, he ran away to sea but, naturally, embarking from South Wales, ended up in Newcastle. From there, he tried to join the circus as a medium but was forced to leave when he got too large. His brief career as an international dope dealer foundered when idiots became freely available on social media. His favourite quality is curiosity, which prevents him from owning cats. He has a number of short stories published in books and anthologies (available through Amazon and Lulu) and in online publications.

Jason McClean is married with two fantastic children that fill up his days with more happiness than he ever thought possible. Name checks for Gaelen and Ariane; not to mention his much loved wife, Lyn. Jason enjoys mountain biking in his spare time and the older he gets the bigger the jumps he is completing. He enjoys riding on the roads as well. With a background in motorcycle journalism (Chief Reporter at Motorcycle News and Editor of Inside Line, the Motorcycle Trade Magazine), Jason wrote the biography of his friend and triple British Superbike Champion John Reynolds, published by Haynes in 2008. Jason is currently writing short stories and building up his voice and writing style for fiction novels. He reads a lot and enjoys thrillers, horror, sci-fi, fantasy and young adult genres. Apart from that, Jason has a job as a Director at www.thepropertyinsurer.co.uk and likes cinema (brief spell as a cinema critic when training as a journalist was one of the best jobs in the world), traveling, theatre, eating out, property investing and meeting interesting new people.

Jayne Osborn is an award-winning, well-known writer of metrical poetry (the stuff that rhymes!) and most of her work is humorous, although she does write in serious mode as well. She has been widely published and many of her poems have appeared in *The Spectator* and *The Oldie* magazines, in addition to numerous anthologies and online journals. Jayne has also judged several poetry competitions, run workshops for writers and has facilitated at poetry conferences in the UK and America; in short, poetry is her life! She's a retired college lecturer and a member of the Northampton Magicians Club.

Elizabeth Parikh, a writer from Lancashire, works as a teacher of Religion and Philosophy in North Bedfordshire. She has a particular penchant for eighties music and writing comedy. Elizabeth first came to love the genre while watching the sitcom *Bottom* as a young girl, and while too young to truly appreciate the genius of vodka margarine, a seed was planted to one day create comedy of her own. She was encouraged as a candidate at the Media Guardian Television Festival where she learnt how to master comedy sketches with writers from Baby Cow Productions and went on to co-write two plays for the Edinburgh Fringe Festival (*Plot Holes and Advert Breaks* and *Murder We Wrote*) which received four star reviews from *Three Weeks* magazine. Elizabeth then worked for five years as a script reader for the Manchester Library Theatre. Elizabeth is also a Member of Directors' Cut Theatre in partnership with Southwark Playhouse. A Britpop-themed comedic monologue, penned by Elizabeth, was performed earlier this year by Not Too Tame Theatre Company. She is also currently working on an audio drama monologue with Theatre503. Recently Elizabeth sold a script, I HEART AMY, to The Wireless Theatre Company, Brighton, which will be produced in 2017.

Michael J Richards is founder Chair of Northants Writers' Ink. In 2015, he edited Northants Writers' Ink first anthology *Tales of the Scorpion* and in 2016, its second, *While Glancing out of a Window*. Both are available on Amazon (paperback and Kindle versions) and other good bookselling websites. He is also Chair of Northampton Literature Group and leads its Writing Circle. He is a Deputy Chair of Northampton Writing Group, a member of Northants Authors and a judge for the H E Bates Short Story Competition. In 2014, he published *Afterwards Our Buildings Shape Us*, a comic horror novella. In 2015, he wrote and directed *The Isolated Essence of a Subject*, a twenty-minute film. In 2017, as well as editing this anthology, he published *Bodies for Sale!*, twenty of his horror, sci-fi and mythic stories, and *Frank Peters: his life, times and crimes*, the true life story of a London criminal. He is now writing a collection of short stories on the theme of male/male relationships.

Allan Shipham is a founder member of the group and continues to take an active role. He works in the construction industry but also finds time for other activities including creative writing. Following feedback from the group's previous anthologies, Allan has continued to explore his creativity and develop his writing skills. In this anthology, he shares pieces that take you on a journey and explore moments in time. He enjoys sharing his pieces of work and seeing the reaction in people's faces.

Chris Wright is an IT analyst and programmer based in Wellingborough. He is married to the long-suffering Karen and has three grown children and two growing grandchildren. With an educational background in maths and computing, he has always had a keen interest in both reading and viewing science fiction. Writing was a later development, science fiction the natural destination. The group has been a great help in developing his skills and broadening the genres that he's willing to tackle. The five short stories in this anthology are his first published works. He is treasurer of Northants Writers' Ink.

Lightning Source UK Ltd.
Milton Keynes UK
UKOW04f0308151117
312700UK00002B/53/P

9 781787 196001